BEYOND
RECOGNITION

BEYOND RECOGNITION

George Kanawaty

BEYOND RECOGNITION

iUniverse books may be ordered through booksellers or by contacting:

iUniverse
1663 Liberty Drive
Bloomington, IN 47403
www.iuniverse.com
844-349-9409

Because of the dynamic nature of the Internet, any web addresses or links contained in this book may have changed since publication and may no longer be valid. The views expressed in this work are solely those of the author and do not necessarily reflect the views of the publisher, and the publisher hereby disclaims any responsibility for them.

Any people depicted in stock imagery provided by Getty Images are models, and such images are being used for illustrative purposes only. Certain stock imagery © Getty Images.

ISBN: 978-1-6632-3685-2 (sc)
ISBN: 978-1-6632-3686-9 (e)

Library of Congress Control Number: 2022904079

Print information available on the last page.

iUniverse rev. date: 03/03/2022

Contents

Dedication

To the people who inspired me to contemplate this novel and to Georgette, Kevin, Shane, Christine, Linda and Sam.

Author's Note

The events portrayed in this novel take place in two countries, the UK and the Philippines, and span two decades beginning in the 1970s. These were trying times for the UK as a new conservative government had launched a program to dismantle public entities such as the Coal Board, British Steel, British Gas, and others, all major employers, and labor unrest ensued.

The Philippines, while struggling to meet development goals, also faced a fundamental insurgency devoted to the establishment of an Islamic state in the southern part of the country. Both situations provided the background for this novel.

While the characters in this novel are fictitious, their actions are woven in nonfiction, real-life settings that highlight present preoccupations and issues including maintaining happiness in marriage, the challenges faced when relocating from one culture to another, and the underlying causes and realities of fundamental insurgency movements.

Till Death Do Us Part

Janet Jones lay in bed eyes wide open and too excited and too happy to sleep. *What will it be like to be called Mrs. Barnes?* she wondered.

She had waited for this day for three years. Deep inside, she knew it was going to happen, and yet, when Andrew had proposed that evening, she had been taken by surprise. She hoped he had not noticed her blush and the tears she was trying to suppress. Her voice had quivered, and her heart had pounded.

She wanted to relive that evening a hundred times over, to recall every word they had spoken at their favorite table in their favorite restaurant, the going and coming of waiters, the chatter and occasional laughter at other tables, the odd mix of aromas—food, cigarette smoke, and burning candles. A befitting background for a marriage proposal.

She glanced at her watch. It was well after midnight. She needed to get some sleep but was not able to command it. She had glanced at the newspaper's headlines that morning—the usual sparring in the British Parliament between the conservatives and Labour, Chris Patten's statements on the future of Hong Kong, an analysis of peace prospects in the Middle East a year after the 1993 Oslo accords ... hardly news that could induce peaceful sleep let alone beautiful dreams.

She smiled as she recalled the small, two-story house in Wales where she had grown up. She remembered the small room upstairs she had shared with her sister and playmate Mary; a bunk bed, a table, two chairs and a cupboard competed for the available space. Next door was her parents' room that contained twin beds, a dresser, a chest of drawers, and a cupboard. In front was another small room that became the sewing and ironing room after her grandmother passed away. The bathroom was next.

Stairs led down to a living room with a fireplace, a bay window overlooking the street, and an alcove with enough room for a dining table and six chairs, and then the kitchen. All in all, it was a typical house in their middle-class neighborhood. Theirs was not a life of luxury—far from it— but it was a happy, carefree life.

She recalled how she and Mary dressed in navy-blue uniforms would run to school every morning greeting people as they went and arriving just minutes and on a few occasions mere seconds before the bell rang. Their lives consisted of doing homework and time and weather permitting skipping rope or playing hopscotch in the small backyard till supper.

She had looked forward with great anticipation to the weekends; on Saturdays, they were allowed to watch children's programs on TV and devote more time to playing with friends.

On Sundays, she and Mary would put on their best dresses and black shoes and go with their parents to mass. A special Sunday meal awaited their return, often a crown of lamb or a roast beef with Yorkshire pudding. Sunday evenings would always be special; their father, Arthur, would read a story to them in bed before kissing them goodnight. There would always be repeated pleas for another story as the first one would always be rated too short.

As Janet reminisced, sadness crossed her face. She had been nine when her father, whose features she vaguely remembered, left home to work in the Philippines. She told her friends not without some pride that the country was halfway around the world from Wales. Her father wrote frequently, and her mother, Lesley, would read them excerpts from his letters whenever they arrived. These were promptly relayed to their friends with the appropriate exaggerations and amplifications fed by their imagination.

One day, tragedy struck. The girls were told by their sobbing mother that their father had died in a car accident. Amid tears, hugs, and motherly reassurances, Mary asked if that meant their father was in heaven and observing them from above. Older Janet knew better. Her father had gone never to be seen or to set eyes on them again.

In time, they began to adjust to the family's new reality. Their mother took over reading them the weekend stories and prodding them to do their homework and go to bed.

Janet's dear sister Mary, her closest friend, was always the dreamer in the family. At age twelve, she had befriended a boy her age who introduced her to classical music. They often lay on the floor holding hands and listening to Rachmaninov, Tchaikovsky, and Mozart. At that early age, she dreamed of pursuing a career in music. She chose the cello as her instrument and practiced every day for hours. At sixteen, Mary was elated to learn that she had been accepted for study at the Academy of St Martin-in-the-Fields. That would improve her chances of joining that prestigious orchestra or other orchestras later. Her life seemed set; she would take her future a step at a time.

For her part, Janet was an avid reader often quoting one author or another and readily expressing her views whenever the occasion arose. At fifteen, she had already made up her mind to become a lawyer. She worked hard to reach that objective, and when at seventeen she was accepted at London University's Faculty of Arts, she was overjoyed.

It was there that she met Andrew, a chance encounter in the crowded cafeteria. She was halfway through her lunch when a person holding a tray asked with some embarrassment, "Forgive me. Is that seat free by any chance? I'm Andrew Barnes."

She motioned him to sit and said, "Hello, I'm Janet Jones. This place gets crowded very quickly."

"It does. I usually try to come earlier, but I was delayed at the library. What are you studying if I may ask?"

"I'm first-year arts, but I intend to go for law."

"Splendid!"

"And yourself?"

"I'm afraid this is my last year of management studies. I would have liked to continue and get a master's, but I can't afford it at present."

Janet threw several glances at him. She admired him the way all fresh, young students admire their seniors, but she also noticed his well-built body, handsome face, reddish-brown hair parted on the side, green eyes, and beautiful, white teeth hiding behind full lips. She had finished eating but waited politely until he finished his meal. He asked if he could offer her coffee or tea, and she opted for the latter. He excused himself and returned with two cups of tea.

"Enjoy your university years while they last," he said with a sigh.

"Why do you say that?"

"Well, university years are fun years despite the pressure of studies and exams. I regret that they will soon be over for me. As a student, I enjoyed the social life, the camaraderie, the sports events, and other activities university life offers. When I thought of a working career, I was quite optimistic feeling for sure that the world would readily embrace me as soon as I got my degree. The closer I got to graduation, however, the more apprehensive I became as word kept spreading about dim job prospects and how difficult it was not only to find but also to hold onto a good job."

"You sound too pessimistic."

"Let's say I'm not overly optimistic. I've become more realistic."

They finished their tea and were pondering their next move when Andrew said, "I do apologize. I feel awful. I did all the talking, crying on your shoulder as I did. You must feel I'm so self-centered. Could we meet again? Perhaps you can then tell me about yourself. After all, I know nothing about you except your name."

Janet thought it over for a few seconds before nodding and blushing and adding that there was really nothing much to reveal about herself.

She fondly remembered their courtship—the joy of anticipation whenever a date was set, the growing friendship and hidden affection they had for each other. She admired his candor and maturity and his willingness to see another person's point of view. He liked music and sports and seemed to have found a balance between academic achievement and social enjoyment. He told her that what he admired about her was her unusual combination of shyness and assertiveness. She was well read and had an inquisitive mind; he liked the way she presented her ideas. No doubt she would make an excellent lawyer he had told her. Unspoken until much later was the strong physical attraction they had for each other.

When Andrew graduated a few months later, there followed a period of heightened anxiety almost bordering on depression as he continued to chase real and more often imaginary job opportunities. Then one day he called her almost too excited to talk. In an exuberant tone, he told her that he had just received an offer from British Airways to work on pricing in their financial department. She was overwhelmed with happiness for both of them as she had come to regard her future as intertwined with his.

The news called for a celebration Andrew had said suggesting an outing to Stratford-on-Avon. There, he rented a boat. It was a beautiful sunny day with scattered white clouds, a perfect day for a slow, aimless rowing. With every stroke of the oar, the calm water released tiny ripples with a hissing sound before the river regained its calm and allowed them to glide farther. As they did so, a light breeze caressed Janet's blackish hair disturbing its order and lifting it slightly off her slender neck. For a long while, Andrew and Janet exchanged only a few words as if afraid to disturb the serenity.

It had been a good ten days since it had last rained, an unusually dry and sunny period. Janet remembered how Andrew broke the silence gesturing to a weeping willow.

"Look at this tree. Isn't it strange? Its branches are touching the water yet it is probably dying of thirst." He paused. "It's like us. We hold hands and touch, but inside, we're burning with desire for each other. I love you more than I can express. I want to be with you every moment. You've become such a part of me, Janet. I cannot imagine life without you."

They left the boat and kissed again and again as they lay side by side day on the lawn daydreaming.

As they drifted back to London, Janet needed little persuasion to join him in his small flat.

"Would you like a drink?" he asked.

"No thank you, but a cup of tea would be fine. Let me put on the kettle, and I'll freshen up in the meantime."

She sat on the floor beside him sipping tea before resting her face on his lap. Andrew gently pulled her toward him. With their lips locked, he moved her slowly to his bed. One hand had slipped under her skirt to caress her thighs. She had allowed that much before but always pushed his hands gently away whenever he attempted to feel her breasts. But she found herself lying on his bed and dragging him over her, and when he placed his hands on her breasts, she offered no resistance. He slowly began to undress her and himself. It was the first time he had seen her bare breasts.

"They're far lovelier than I imagined them to be," he said feeling their smooth firmness. Janet felt his lips straying on her neck and moving slowly down to take over from where his hand had been. Excited as she was, she kept pondering a point—Should she tell him or let him find out for himself? She took his face in her hands and said, "Andrew, darling, I want you to know … I'm still a virgin."

He tried to move away from her, but she would not let

him. Her legs were wrapped around him, and her hands were clasping his back firmly. "I want you, Andrew."

"We can still—"

"No, no. I want you inside me."

"Are you sure?"

"Yes I am."

Janet remembered how later with a deep sigh he had said, "What a perfect ending for a perfect day. No regrets?"

She, with beads of sweat on her forehead and her body throbbing with pain and pleasure, had responded with a hug and said, "None. None whatsoever."

It was their first of infrequent sexual encounters. She had told him once, "Let's leave something to look forward to when and if we get married assuming I'll say yes when you propose."

Life went on. Hardly a day passed when they did not phone or see each other. Andrew described to her the intricacies of the airline business, which fascinated him. His dream came true when two years later, he won a competition to transfer to the Planning Department. Work there would be more interesting, he had told her, for it involved planning routes, schedules, fleet replacement, alliances with other airlines, and prospects for further expansion.

Janet kept him abreast with her progress and other university events. She relayed to him on occasion what she learned of the nuances and varying interpretations attached to some legal instruments and some landmark cases she found interesting. At twenty-two, she ended her studies with honors.

Then the big event of that cold, damp, and foggy evening in October 1994, which will remain engraved in her memory. He took her out to their favorite restaurant and ordered a bottle of champagne. She looked at him a bit startled and asked, "What are we celebrating? Don't tell me you got another promotion."

"No. This is far more important. I've made a very serious decision," he said raising his glass and looking her in the eye. "I decided to get married."

Trying hard to conceal her surprise, she pretended to sidestep the issue.

"And who is this most unfortunate bride-to-be?"

"I'm talking to her right now."

"Is this a proposal?" she asked with a grin.

"But of course."

"You have to do better than that, Andrew. After all, a girl gets proposed to once and if she's lucky twice in her lifetime!"

"Fine. Let me try again, Janet darling." He was smiling broadly. "After chasing you for a good part of three years, I give up. Now how would you like to become Mrs. Barnes?"

"Mrs. Barnes! I'm not sure I like that. I prefer Jones. I could consider it if I'm called Jones-Barnes or Barnes-Jones or stay simply Jones."

"No way. I want you body, soul, and name."

They were enjoying this teasing game, but Andrew's smile faded and he adopted a more serious tone. "Seriously, sweetheart. I'll be the happiest man in the world if you'll marry me. Will you?"

Janet looked at him for a few seconds. Tears were welling up in her eyes. She stood and stretched her arms toward him. "Of course I will, Andrew darling."

Despite the curious looks from other diners, they kissed passionately before settling down again. "I'll even accept being called Mrs. Barnes." They laughed.

Their waiter stopped by. "Am I to offer birthday wishes?" he asked with a smile.

Janet smiled at him. "No. Better. We're getting married!"

As word spread to some curious diners, several stopped by their table to offer their congratulations.

"I've been doing some thinking," Andrew said. "We could get married during the Christmas recess and go away for our honeymoon. I can get a free ticket, and as my wife, yours will cost next to nothing. We can travel to the States, perhaps to California, or to the Far East—Hong Kong or Singapore? And we can have one or two stops somewhere along the way. What do you think?"

"Traveling that far? That would be fantastic. I've always wanted to go to the United States, see Los Angeles, San Francisco, and New York. On the other hand, the Far East is also a very attractive proposition. If I recall correctly, Hong Kong will revert to Chinese rule in 1997. I'd like to see it before then. Let's go to Hong Kong. Where else can we stop?"

"Bangkok, Manila, Singapore."

"Manila! I'd love to go to the Philippines."

"Bangkok with its pagodas may be more interesting."

"Perhaps, but ever since I was young, I've dreamed of going to the Philippines. You know my father is buried there, on the island of Mindanao. A car accident. He was only thirty when he died." She paused. "I was just nine when he left. I have only a vague recollection of what he looked like." Sadness crossed her face. "My mother used to read his letters to Mary and me. He had a lot to say about the country and the people, and I used to relay some of these stories to my friends often doctored up to make them more interesting and to give him the halo of a hero.

"I had visions of him returning loaded with gifts and more stories to tell. I wanted to know more about the country and the people he met. How many islands were there, and how many did he visit? Did he ever venture into a forest and see wild animals? Did he make many friends? What were the people like? I had visions of listening to him for days. Alas! That was not to be. Ever since I was young, I learned all I could about the Philippines. I'd really love to see it."

"I understand. Let's go to Hong Kong and Manila then. British Airways covers both cities. I'll start making reservations."

"Oh Andrew, I'm so happy. I really adore you. I have a feeling that everything is going for us. We'll have such a happy life together."

"Well, we can start right now. How will we end this delightful evening? Your place or mine?"

"Both." She knew what he was alluding to. "Not until you walk the aisle! We're only engaged you know." Her smile was radiant. He threw his arms up in despair. It was close to eleven when he took her home.

Janet glanced at the bedside clock once more. It was now close to one. It suddenly dawned on her that she had yet to call her mother and sister to relay the good news. She decided to do so at once disregarding the late hour.

The lengthy, jovial chat with her mother, Lesley, brought up more questions than she had answers for. What plans did she have for invitations, and the reception, the flowers, the wedding dress? On and on. She felt overwhelmed, almost panicky. She needed more time to think things over. One thing she was sure of. She wanted Mary for her bridesmaid, and she told her sister and mother so. She welcomed the opportunity to go over for lunch that weekend to sort matters out. Andrew would come along too she told her mother.

It was shortly past noon on the Sunday when Janet and Andrew arrived at her mother's place. Mary was already there. Lesley and her stepfather, David, gave them warm hugs and exchanged kisses with Janet.

"Congratulations! You kept us guessing for a long time. We're so happy for you!"

"We liked the suspense," Andrew said with a smile and a handshake.

It was Mary's turn. "Oh Janet, you look so radiant!" she said as she hugged her sister.

"Let's all have a good drink," interjected David. "Is it the same? Whisky and water, Andrew, and a sherry for you, Janet?"

"Yes please," they replied.

"It will be an hour before dinner is ready, and a very special dinner it will be," said Lesley. "We have time for a chat. Where do we start?"

For a good hour, they talked about the wedding arrangements, and they continued their discussion over dinner. Lesley had prepared a roast leg of lamb, roast potatoes, and creamed spinach. David had opened a bottle of a Spanish red wine from the Ribera del Duero region; it had a deep ruby color, a great bouquet, and a slightly lingering fruity aftertaste. The aroma of the meal whetted everybody's appetite. A lovely trifle was served for dessert.

"Why don't you make yourself comfortable in the living room," Lesley said. "Janet and I will clear up and prepare the coffee. Besides, both of us have something to discuss that you men shouldn't be involved in."

"I can guess. It must be the wedding dress," said Andrew.

"Whatever it is, it's between the two of us. Come on, Janet, off to the kitchen."

They had hardly started washing the dishes when Lesley said, "Janet, there's a subject I want to raise with you in private. Your father left you and Mary some money in his will. It's being invested with a trust company and is due to you once you turn twenty-five or get married."

"Mother! You never told me that! My father?" Janet exclaimed. "That's a surprise!"

"He wanted it kept secret until it was due lest you girls spent it foolishly. I know that wouldn't have happened, but I had to respect his wishes. It amounts to ten thousand pounds for each of you, and with accumulated interest, the amount should be much higher."

"How generous and thoughtful! I always remember him as a wonderful man. Isn't it tragic to die so young and be buried so far away? And incidentally, Mom, Andrew and I are going to Manila on our honeymoon. Maybe we can visit his grave."

"That would be a silly thing to do. You'll be on your honeymoon. Why would you want to drag death and sadness into it? Just go and enjoy yourself wherever you go."

"But, Mom, he's my father. Don't get me wrong. David has been more than a father to me, but there is my real father leaving me this money and I won't even bother putting a flower on his grave when I am in the same country?"

"Let bygones be bygones, Janet. It's twelve years or more since he passed away. Look at the future. Don't be burdened or saddened by the past at perhaps the happiest time of your life. And why Manila? Why don't you visit other cities instead?"

"I know that he worked and died in Mindanao. Andrew and I were looking at the map. Mindanao looks like a big island. Do you know where he's buried? Maybe you have the name of the organization he worked for in the Philippines or his last address."

Lesley shook her head. "I destroyed all the papers and his letters when we moved to Southampton. It was a big move, and I got rid of a lot of things that had accumulated."

"I really have nothing of him except his photo taken with me and Mary before he left for overseas. How I wish he was still alive and would give me away at my wedding."

"Let's not dwell on this subject any more, Janet. Let's join the others before the coffee gets cold. Wasting your time in Manila would be a big mistake, I'm saying. In the meantime, as soon as you have your wedding certificate, I'll call the solicitor. He's in London. You can see him, and he'll make the arrangements for you with the trust company."

Lesley and Janet joined the others. Over coffee, they rehashed some of the points they had discussed earlier fine-tuning certain details before the discussion drifted to more-mundane matters. Andrew looked at his watch. It was time to leave, he said, if they wanted to avoid the rush hour back to London.

On the way to London, Janet told Andrew about the inheritance. "I wonder if it was intuition that something was going to happen to him that inspired my father to set up this trust fund. It's sad, isn't it? Here he is buried in a foreign country for over twelve years now and probably nobody ever visited him. Andrew darling, do you think we can go and lay flowers on his grave, a token of appreciation for the good father he was and for what he left us? I know he's buried in Mindanao, but where exactly I don't know. There shouldn't be a problem for us to catch a flight there from Manila I presume. Maybe we can go and return the same day or spend one or two days exploring that island. What do you think?"

Andrew nodded. "Sure, we can go if you wish."

"If only we knew the name of the town or had any clue as to where he's buried. My mother told me she couldn't help me on that score. She said she destroyed all his letters when we moved to Southampton. I thought she was acting a bit strange today trying to persuade me to forget the past and to discourage me from going to the Philippines. You don't suppose she didn't get along with him, do you?"

"You told me once that your father worked for a church organization in the Philippines. If we can get to them, they'll tell us where to look. How could he have possibly got in touch with such an organization in a faraway country? Did he respond to a newspaper advertisement?"

"No, no," exclaimed Janet. "I distinctly remember Fr. Timothy of our church having something to do with finding him that job. That's brilliant, Andrew. Fr. Timothy left the parish I believe two or three years ago. I'm sure I can trace him. He could put us on to the Philippines organization. I'll phone him and see what I can find out."

Two days later, Janet was beaming as she announced to Andrew that they had an address, that of Fr. Ramos in Manila, for whose parish her father had worked. Andrew suggested she write to alert him as to the purpose of their visit. That subject was then abruptly dropped as attention focused on the forthcoming wedding set for December 15, 1994.

That December day turned out to be sunny but crispy cold. A light winter breeze had chased the clouds away but left a sustained chill in the air. When Janet walked the aisle with one arm tucked into David's arm and the other holding a cascading bouquet of flowers, the wedding march reverberating from the church organ gave her goose bumps. Gradually, as the service progressed, she began to feel more at ease. Andrew helped lighten the atmosphere by whispering words of affection to her.

It was time to exchange vows; she repeated sentence for sentence what the priest prompted her to say including "Till death do us part." *How ironic*, she thought. *That one phrase can bear two meanings—happiness and sadness at the same time, for is it not death that separates people, yet in the context of the vow, nothing can convey a message of lasting love than this phrase.*

When the priest finally proclaimed, "I now pronounce you man and wife. You may kiss the bride," all the tension Janet felt melted away. She could now receive the kisses and congratulations of her guests.

The newlyweds had reserved their favorite restaurant for the reception. They had had it decorated with flowers and arranged for a three-man band to liven up the occasion. As gallons of wine were consumed over dinner, several toasts were proposed. Loud cheers followed as the bride and groom took to the dance floor joined by young and old.

It was shortly after one in the morning when the newlyweds took leave from the few remaining hard-core invitees.

"One more dance," exclaimed Andrew as they got into their apartment. He put on some soft dance music. "And I want a kiss that lasts the whole tune."

"How could I protest? You now own me body and soul totally and irrevocably," Janet giggled.

He carried her to bed both feeling a bit tipsy. The ecstasy of love left them even more content and relaxed. Soon, they fell into a deep sleep …

Janet was the first to wake up. "Hey, wake up," she said as she climbed over him. "You're burned out on our first day of marriage!"

"Give me a chance. The alcohol has yet to evaporate from my brain."

"You don't make love with your brain, do you?"

"I didn't know you were a sex maniac. All along, I thought you were prudish. Don't forget we have a plane to catch. Planes don't wait, you know. What time is it?"

Janet looked at her watch. "Time enough for another one. We don't have to leave here for a couple of hours."

Flight BA 031 bound for Hong Kong left Heathrow on time at 2:45 p.m. and arrived twelve hours later. They napped occasionally during the flight and felt they could do with more rest, but curiosity and excitement drove them out of their hotel to the streets. It was only around noon Hong Kong time on a sunny, bright, warm day.

The city was breathtaking. Many tall modern buildings mushroomed among other less pretentious ones hugging the mountainous terrain. Thousands of flashy signs in Chinese and English adorned shops, restaurants, and hotels.

Heavy traffic including double-decker buses clogged the streets. Crowds moved swiftly as if everyone was late for an appointment. Many embarked and disembarked from tens of ferries traveling to and from Kowloon, Macau, and other smaller islands. In certain areas, rows of sampans were moored alongside one another serving as permanent homes for poorer families.

Janet and Andrew spent their time sampling food, browsing shops, and visiting some of Hong Kong's landmarks. They took a day trip to Kowloon and another to Macau. Before they knew it, it was time to board the plane for their next destination, Manila.

Manila was a very different city with a charm of its own, more spread out, adorned with green spaces, less-conspicuous tall buildings, and hectic traffic but of a different nature than Hong Kong as cars, buses, motorcycles, and shiny and elaborately decorated tricycle taxis competed for road space. As their stay there would be short, they quickly got an appointment with Fr. Ramos.

Dressed in blue jeans and a short-sleeved shirt with a wooden cross hanging around his neck, Fr. Ramos greeted them warmly and put them at ease almost instantly. After the usual niceties, he addressed the subject that brought them together; he had effusive praise for Janet's father. He told them that Arthur was buried in Kipagah, a small town in the southeastern part of the island of Mindanao.

"Actually, I met your father only once," he told them, "when he first arrived. I recall how eager he was to start his assignment. Through his reports and the feedback I got from Mindanao, I knew of the excellent job he did, which made me very happy. When I heard the sad news, I flew over, and together with a local priest, Fr. Angel, we officiated at his funeral. Many of his students attended.

"Poor Fr. Angel. He had been in poor health for a while and became forgetful with age. He took his retirement a year ago I understand. But if you're planning to go there, I could have Rony accompany you if you wish. He accompanied your late father during his first six months on the island. He could be your guide and arrange for your plane tickets and for ground transportation. He works for the parish part time. Internal flights in the Philippines are rather cheap, and if you don't mind paying for his ticket, I can get in touch with him right away."

"That would be wonderful," Janet said. "We'd certainly appreciate that. We'll have no problem covering his expenses."

Andrew and Janet enjoyed Rony's company. With his everlasting smile and obliging manner, he had offered to show them Manila and took them shopping prior to their departure to Mindanao. He spoke at length about Arthur and their six months together on the island when he had accompanied him many years earlier. He talked about Arthur's work, which consisted of training people living in rural areas in skills that could enable them to augment their income. He told them how much Janet's father was appreciated by his students and how he often spoke about his family in Wales. Unfortunately, he added, the person who arrived to replace him did not live up to expectations having succumbed on several occasions to the charm of Filipina girls. This had brought complaints from the local people and problems for the parish. That would have never happened with Arthur, he assured them.

"I understand my father died in a car accident. How did this happen? Was it a head-on collision?"

"No. He apparently went off the road. The car overturned and burst into flames. I was told he was burned beyond recognition."

"How awful!" Janet said covering her face with her hands.

"He must have died instantly and did not suffer," Rony added.

The flight to Davao in Mindanao was comfortable. On arrival, Rony made arrangements with a taxi driver to stay with them for as long as they wanted having hired him by the hour. A two-hour drive brought them to their destination, Kipagah. Rony started showing them points of interest on the way, but noting Janet's silence and pensive mood, he fell silent. They stopped to buy some flowers on the way.

The ornate iron gates of the cemetery were shut. Flaking black paint revealed rusty metal. Janet saw a spiderweb glistening in the sun on top of the gate. Rony pushed the heavy gate, which yielded slowly with a groan. A few minutes later, a thin, old man, a guard with a pale face and hollow, inquiring eyes walked up. He looked like a dead man warmed over. In response to their query, he walked slowly through the maze of slab stones, and they followed. Some tombs were very ornate with statues of angels and pictures of the deceased while others were simpler. He stopped and pointed to a plain cement slab with the image of a cross and the words "Arthur Jones 1952–1981 May he rest in peace." The gray slab was mostly covered by green moss and surrounded by weeds and grass.

The three of them stood by the grave in silence. Janet and Rony laid down their flowers. Soon, Janet was overcome by emotions and began to sob. The talk about the accomplishments of her father, his tragic death, and this lonely, neglected tomb in a faraway country was too much to bear. She tried remembering what she could of him from her childhood and tried to control her emotions, but she broke down in grief. Andrew held her hand. They stood there for fifteen minutes before they finally made a move to leave. Andrew gave the guard some money asking him to clean the slab and plant flowers around it.

"I wonder what his last days were like," Janet said as she wiped her tears.

"Maybe we can find out where he lived and speak to the people there. He must have rented a place somewhere in this town. It would have been easy if Fr. Angel were around, but I have no clue where he retired to, and even if I did, with Alzheimer's, he probably wouldn't remember much."

They walked away in silence. Andrew wanted to diffuse the tension and alleviate his wife's sadness. "We have two hours before starting on our way back to Davao. Perhaps we should explore the town."

"On second thought," Rony said, "we can inquire at the parish. Knowing Arthur, he probably was a regular churchgoer here. In these small towns, everybody seems to know everybody, and a foreigner living here would be easily remembered I should think."

Janet looked at Andrew with pleading eyes. "Andrew darling, I know this isn't pleasant for you, but since we're here, can we just try this once?"

"Surely. I'm easy."

They were driven to the parish. Rony went inside alone. A few minutes later, he emerged to tell them that the secretary of the parish remembered Arthur and the funeral because of the circumstances surrounding his death. The secretary did not know where he had lived but remembered his being friendly with Miguel Diaz, a member of the church who owned a garage in town. It was Miguel who had come to see them to discuss the funeral arrangements.

A visit to a nearby garage yielded nothing. They decided to try one more time. Their taxi pulled into a gas station with an adjoining garage. Rony went to speak to someone operating the pump; they saw the worker shake his head. Just as Rony was heading toward them, a car pulled in and a man in overalls stepped out and talked to Rony. Andrew and Janet figured out that he must be the garage owner.

When Rony returned, he told them that the owner knew Miguel Diaz well. He also remembered the Englishman who had rented a place in Miguel's house. However, Miguel had since sold his business and moved to Manila. The garage owner knew where Miguel had lived and gave the taxi driver the directions. Maybe they could just drive there and have a look, Rony suggested.

It was not far. The taxi wove its way through winding roads and alleys before reaching an unpretentious street. The driver pointed to a modest two-story building. They stepped out. Andrew commented that the place was probably more spacious inside; appearances were often deceiving. They saw Rony slip into a nearby garage to talk to its owner. He soon returned to report to them what he had found out. The place he visited used to be Miguel's garage. Miguel, his wife, his brother, and his sister had all moved to Manila some time ago, but Miguel's mother still lived in that house.

"Maybe we should move on now that we've seen the place," said Andrew.

"We could knock at the door and speak to Mrs. Diaz," said Rony. "I'm sure that if you tell her you'd like to see the place your father rented, she'll let you in. Filipinos are very hospitable, and they welcome foreigners."

Without waiting for an answer, he knocked at the door. A woman in her sixties opened the door cautiously and greeted them with a surprised look.

"Mrs. Diaz?" said Janet, "I hope I'm not disturbing you. I'm Janet Barnes, and this is my husband, Andrew, and our friend, Rony."

The woman nodded with a broad smile and opened the door wider.

"Did Mr. Arthur Jones live here some time ago?" asked Janet.

The woman drew a blank for a few seconds. "Arthur? No … No Arthur … Arturo yes, oh, a long time … very long time ago."

"We're talking about Arthur, an Englishman."

"Not here. Arturo, yes, but he is away." Mrs. Diaz waved her hand as if to signal that he was far away.

To clear up any misunderstanding, Janet produced the picture of her father with her and Mary. "This is him, and this is me. I'm his daughter."

The smile dried on the woman's face. She appeared confused. "Sorry, I made mistake. Not here."

Rony started talking to the woman in Tagalog. She shook her head, said, "Excuse me," and closed the door.

They backed away, Janet bewildered and Andrew perplexed.

"Crazy woman," said Rony. "I told her you came from England and wanted to see where your father had lived."

"I swear she recognized the picture, but as soon as I said I was his daughter, she clamped down."

"She was referring to Arturo," said Rony.

"But isn't that Spanish for Arthur?"

"Pay no attention to what she said. She didn't sound balanced to me," said Rony.

"But what did she mean saying he was away when we just visited his grave?"

"My dear Janet, you read too many Agatha Christie books. As Rony said, the woman sounded incoherent. Maybe she has Alzheimer's."

But Janet had questions. *Who is this Arturo who's away? Is the woman really incoherent?* She was nonetheless happy to have visited her father's grave. *You won't be forgotten, Dad.* She decided not to raise the subject again. As her mother had told her, she was on her honeymoon and should enjoy it.

Back in Manila, they bid Rony goodbye and thanked him profusely.

Two days later, they boarded the plane to London loaded with gifts for family and friends and with souvenirs for their apartment.

Arthur

He spent a fitful night. It must have been around four in the morning when he finally went into a deep sleep only to be awakened three hours later with a cup of morning tea and a nudge from his wife, Lesley.

"Time you got up. Have some tea, love. Good morning."

He murmured a good morning, but before he could collect his thoughts, she added, "Big day for you, isn't it?"

He nodded and sipped his tea. He struggled half-asleep to get ready. A hot bath woke him up. He got dressed, and he lifted the window curtain slightly to look down at the street. He saw a few people clad in coats and scarves walking briskly. *Another damp, cold, and gray day*, he thought. It was only mid-September, but winter seemed eager to make its presence felt. *But what does it matter anyhow?* He was leaving his home and his country that morning.

Before he could lose himself further in his thoughts, a shout from Lesley reminded him that his eggs were getting cold. That was the usual second reminder. Over the years, he had come to ignore her first call announcing that breakfast was ready and responded more readily to her second call that things were getting cold. On her side, she had been calling him and their two daughters, Janet and Mary, for breakfast five minutes before it was actually ready so that a second call would get everybody to the table in time for a hot meal.

Arthur sat for breakfast. Silence was broken once in a while by a request for someone to pass the toast or butter. Not that this was a very talkative family, but normally, nine-year-old Janet and seven-year-old Mary would have something to say about school, their teachers, or their friends or sometimes would tease each other. But that morning, hardly any words were uttered. Arthur looked at his two girls and wondered what they would look like when he returned in two years.

Lesley broke the silence. "You're going to be late for school. Come on, give your dad a kiss and say goodbye."

Mary dashed to her father, gave him a big hug, and looked up at him with wet eyes. "You'll write, won't you, Dad?"

"Of course I will. I'll tell you all about it."

It was Janet's turn. She allowed a tear to roll down her cheek. Pressing her wet cheek against his and with a kiss and a hug, she said, "Take care, Dad. Don't forget to tell us about the plane ride as well."

"And you take care of yourselves and be good to Mom. She'll need your help while I'm away."

"I'll miss you a lot, Dad," shouted Mary as she waved goodbye.

"Me too, Dad!" added Janet.

The girls ran off to school. Arthur had been struggling to keep his emotions under control. He loved his girls dearly. Their hugs meant a lot to him. He wished he had hugged and kissed them more often, but somehow, his rather conservative upbringing frowned on too much expressed emotions.

He began to wonder if he had made the right decision. Two years away from his family was a long time. Why did he allow himself to be carried away embarking on an adventure that would take him far from his family and customary way of life? He could very well have continued leading his usual routine, and that day would have been like any other. Gone was the early enthusiasm he had had for this assignment. It had been gradually replaced by a sense of apprehension and fear of the unknown.

"Will you load the car, love?" Lesley asked him. Without waiting for his reaction, she glanced at her watch. "I should drive you to the railway station in fifteen minutes. Time enough for me to tidy up."

Arthur put his two suitcases in the trunk and looked at his watch. The drive to the train station was short. They arrived ten minutes before the 8:50 train to London. He looked at her. Many times, he longed to go away alone, but now that this was happening, he hated to part with her. She represented continuity and stability in his life. Leaving Lesley was crossing the threshold of the known to the unknown. He wanted to hang on longer. As the train appeared in the distance, he hugged her passionately. "I'll miss you, Les. I love you, you know."

She responded with an affectionate and tight hug and kiss. "You haven't told me that you loved me in a long time. Take care of yourself, and watch those Filipina girls," she said half- jokingly. It was a joke all right, she thought, for Arthur was such a bashful and loyal husband. There was no way whatsoever he would go astray.

He did not know how to respond, but he kissed her again and again. He was fighting back a tear while she began to sob. He got on the train, and they continued waving to each other as the train pulled out. After a final wave, Arthur sat and tried to read the newspaper he had brought with him, but somehow, the news items did not register. He was apprehensive, anxious, and nervous. This was the first time he was leaving England except for honeymooning in Ireland. He and Lesley had driven to the coast and took a ferry to Ireland, Baltimore Town in County Cork. It was a beautiful spot—a tiny harbor, lush, green surroundings, and Cape Clear Island a short distance away. Ireland was another country. People may have been a bit different. He found them to be open, fun loving, and hospitable. They enjoyed a good drink and a good laugh. Yet the similarities he thought outweighed the differences. The Irish spoke English albeit with a different accent and drove on the same side of the road. The weather was similar if not a shade wetter than Wales.

But this was a different trip. He had accepted a two-year assignment in the Philippines, where everything would be different—people, language, habits, and culture to say nothing of the weather. He was leaping into the unknown. Adding to his anxiety was the fact that he had never been on a plane before. He had discreetly inquired from experienced friends and was rehearsing in his mind what he should do on arriving in London. He was to take the underground from Reading Station to Heathrow Airport, a forty-five minute ride, check in with British Airways, and get to his gate.

He arrived in London and soon found himself in Heathrow's terminal 4 over two hours before departure. Alternating between pacing the floor and sitting, he kept looking at his watch. Fully an hour before departure, he headed to his gate area, sat, and examined his boarding pass for the sixth time trying to ascertain that he was sitting by the right gate and memorizing his seat number.

An hour later, passengers on flight BA 031 were invited to board the flight bound for Hong Kong and Manila on that chilly morning of September 12, 1980. His seat was 32 C, an aisle seat in the Boeing 747. It would be almost twelve hours to their first destination, Hong Kong, and an additional two hours to Manila, the steward announced.

After takeoff, Arthur listened to various announcements and watched the stewardesses pass out newspapers, earphones, and menus and offering drinks. He asked for a whisky and water and was ready to pay for it but then noticed that no other passengers did. Soon, lunch and wine were served followed by liquors. He sipped his cognac slowly. He felt a bit more relaxed and rather drowsy. He closed his eyes but was too excited to sleep. Several thoughts flashed through his mind and just as quickly faded away. He pushed his reclining seat back, felt more comfortable, and began to reminisce about his life.

He had been born twenty-nine years earlier in a small mining town in County Glamorganshire in South Wales. Following in his grandfather's path, his father worked in the coal mines since his teens and shortly thereafter married his mother. Arthur was the third child following two sisters. Ever since he was five, his father would explain to him with a sense of pride the work of a miner. Little Arthur asked lots of questions about the way the shafts were dug, how the explosives worked, and how the coal was brought to the surface. His mother went to work soon after he was born to help support their growing family; she helped at a grocery store for a few hours a week and took in laundry and ironing. There was no shortage of single people in town who were happy to unload their dirty laundry at their house particularly at the modest prices his mother charged.

But attending to the needs of a family, managing a home, working, and keeping laundry deadlines slowly but surely wore her down. She developed black lines under her eyes, and she looked haggard. While she made sure that her children were properly dressed and the house was tidy and neat, she had no time to look after her own appearance.

Sundays were an exception. His mother was a devout Catholic, and Arthur attended Sunday school for as long as he could remember. Later, he joined the boys' choir, and at age eight had his first communion. He distinctly remembered that day. His mother had baked a cake, and a few friends came over after the service. He received three presents—a Bible, which he always kept and had brought with him on this trip, a rosary, and a silver cross and chain. But above all, he remembered that day, for it was the first time he had put on long pants and wore a tie. He remembered hanging onto both items not wanting to part with them until it was time for bed.

A year later, an incident took place that seemed to have changed the course of his life. He was at school. It was 3:40 in the afternoon with twenty minutes to go before the end of the school day. Suddenly, a siren began to wail. The teacher froze. The children gave each other perplexed looks. "Class dismissed!" the teacher snapped and rushed outside.

In the school corridor, he learned what the siren meant … An accident at the mine. He ran home. "Where's Mom? There's an accident at the mine!" he told one of his sisters.

"She left to go there."

"I'm going too."

"Wait. I'm coming with you."

Hand in hand, they walked briskly to the mine. The streets had emptied, but the siren was still blowing and getting louder as they approached the site. It was a good forty minutes before they faced a scene that he would always remember. Hundreds of anxious and gloomy men and women had gathered with their eyes glued on the shaft entrance. Some were sobbing, and others were whispering to each other in somber tones.

The children found their mother and stuck close to her. Suddenly, two men wearing yellow helmets shouted, "Make way! Make way!" The crowd pressed against each other to clear a path and stretched their necks to get a good look. An elevator door opened, and six men bearing a stretcher appeared. He recognized his father as one of the bearers. The body on the stretcher was covered. There was a gasp in the crowd. Anxious people wanted to know the dead man's identity. His mother wiping a tear hugged them. "What are you doing here anyway? This is no place for children. Let's go home."

When their father showed up later that night tired and pained, his mother knew better than to ask him questions. She would get the full details the following day at the grocery store.

The silence was broken by an outburst coming from the father: "Bugger the government! Bugger the Coal Board! Bugger it all! These lads never stood a chance." He grabbed young Arthur by the shoulders. "Don't you ever work in a coal mine when you grow up, son."

Arthur heard his mother say, "Amen."

His father set off for a drink at the Swan, a pub not far down the road.

Ever since that incident, his father's visits to the pub

became more frequent and ended up being daily. Gradually, bitterness replaced his father's sense of pride at work. Matters were not helped when in 1979, a conservative government replaced Labour. Margaret Thatcher, the new prime minister, launched a vast program to eliminate "wasteful public practices" through privatization and reduction of subsidies to public corporations. She hammered at the notion that inefficient productive facilities should be phased out. Among other public corporations, British Coal was an obvious target. Soon, the coal mine where his father worked was buzzing with rumors that the pit would soon be closed.

A defiant air prevailed among the miners. They had struck before on many occasions and could do so again. Only that time, things were different. For three years, Thatcher pushed ahead with amendments to the labor law to regulate the striking power of the unions and increase flexibility in the use of manpower. Soon, new management at British Coal announced the closure of several pits including the one in their hometown.

Arthur Scargill, the flamboyant coal miners' union leader, announced an indefinite strike vowing to force the Coal Board management to reverse its decisions. The strike, declared illegal by the government, led to nasty confrontations between the strikers and the police. Dozens were injured on both sides every day with no end in sight. Young Arthur's father was dividing his time almost equally between the picket lines and the pub. He was injured twice during the first six months.

Several months later, as the confrontation dragged on, the strike funds began to dry up. The strikers became gloomy and demoralized. The numbers showing up at picket lines gradually shrunk. Then one day, his father collapsed—a victim of a heart attack brought on by several decades of arduous work and heavy smoking and drinking. The stress brought on by job loss and daily confrontations also helped seal his fate.

At age sixteen, Arthur enrolled in a vocational school for a three-year course in mechanical trades. He hoped to find a job in a factory somewhere after graduation as a semiskilled or a skilled worker or in a maintenance outfit. In the meantime, his older sister, who had married a coal miner, had moved to Newcastle with her husband.

The second sister soon followed moving to the Midlands as a result of marrying an owner of a small tobacco and newspaper shop. Both weddings had taken place a few months before his father's death. Arthur found himself alone at home with his mother. Their income had shrunk, but there were fewer mouths to feed.

At school, Arthur excelled in his studies, and he rarely joined his colleagues for a beer at the pub. He continued to be active in church affairs and in a sense lived up to what his mother inspired him to be—a person with high moral values.

Six months before graduation, Arthur sat down to a cup of tea with his mother. He was in a pensive and gloomy mood.

"What's on your mind, son?"

"Mom, I've been making discreet inquiries about the job market. Things don't look good. In fact, they look downright bleak. Very few companies are hiring inexperienced graduates like us. Fewer still in places like this town. Ever since the mine closed, this town has joined the ranks of the so-called depressed areas.

"The situation with coal mining is not unique you know. Some thirty thousand workers were let go by British Steel, and you have the same scenario with British Gas, British Telecom, and so on. Most of these companies offer programs to counsel and retrain the labor they lay off, and some subsidize the initial employment of their workers with other firms. They pay part of the salaries for the first year to any employer who takes on their redundant workers. This is the type of competition we young, inexperienced graduates are coming up against. But that's not all.

"New, intelligent machines and equipment are being developed all the time. Things like robots and computers that are reducing the need for labor. We're competing with intelligent machines, Mom. Things are happening so fast that I sometimes wonder whether our curriculum at school is becoming irrelevant. Our government keeps telling us that the depression is over, that the economy is gradually improving, but mark my words, Mom. Even if that really happens, companies won't hire more people. They'll buy better machines instead."

His mother listened intently but did not quite grasp the meaning of these complicated words he used such as robots, nor could she comprehend what he said about competition with machines. How can machines be intelligent? But she perfectly well concurred with what he said about the depression and their town being economically depressed. After the mine closed, many families moved out. Her job at the grocery store was terminated. Fewer clients brought in their laundry. She took on additional odd jobs like mending clothes or knitting socks and scarves. Arthur also helped. Through Fr. Timothy, he found a summer job as an assistant mechanic at a garage; that earned him some money and gave him insight into car mechanics.

"Don't worry about the future, Arthur. So far, we've coped, haven't we?"

"I have to worry about the future. The principal of the school likes me. I went to see him today for advice. He seemed to agree with my assessment of the job prospects, but then he asked me if I was interested in a teaching job. I hadn't thought about that. It would require four more years of study—three years at a higher technical institute and one year of pedagogical training. He felt certain that my grades would facilitate my admission to the technical institute, and he said he'd write a letter of recommendation. What do you think, Mom?"

"But of course you should go for it," she said. Sensing what was on his mind, she added, "We'll manage … Don't worry."

Arthur's becoming a teacher rather than a worker was a wonderful prospect in her mind. It would lift them financially and in social status she figured. But she was also elated because Arthur had confided in her sharing his thoughts and anxieties. She decided the moment was ripe to bring up a subject that had been on her mind for a while. "I saw you talking with the Slater girl at church last Sunday. You know the one, Lesley. She's a nice girl, isn't she?"

"Yes she is, but Mom, it's just the usual niceties. There's nothing to it."

"Your sisters got married when they were eighteen and nineteen. Your father married when he was twenty. You're eighteen. You shouldn't put it off for long, son."

"But I've just finished explaining to you the work

situation. I could still have four more years of study ahead of me."

"That should be no obstacle. You can live in this house, and if your wife works, that would help. I just want to say that if you decide on Lesley, I'll be very pleased. She comes from a good Christian family."

She stood and bent over and gave him a kiss on the cheek, something she had not done for a long time. Arthur did not respond. He had known Lesley for many years but had never thought of her as a prospective wife. But he began pondering that possibility. Lesley was not what you would call a stunning beauty by any stretch of the imagination. She was well built, not exactly stout but not thin either. She had hazel eyes and brownish hair and had blemishes on her cheeks. She was slightly shorter than he was. Her overall appearance could be summed up as a plain, wholesome Welsh girl. She hardly used any makeup, and like him, she attended mass every Sunday. He thought that maybe he should get to know her better.

Several weeks later and after much hesitation, while they were leaving church, he gathered his courage and asked her for tea at a tearoom nearby. She readily accepted. They talked about many things for a good hour before he walked her home. They repeated this encounter a couple of weeks later except that that time, he told her of his plans to pursue further studies to become an instructor. She was happy for him and told him that she too had good prospects of becoming a teacher at a primary school when she graduated a month later.

"The school will be giving a graduation dance on that occasion."

"Are you going?"

"Nobody's offered to accompany me yet."

He blushed, hesitated, and stumbled for words. "Can I escort you then?"

"Oh Arthur! That would be smashing."

The graduation dance was a joyful, noisy affair. Everybody seemed to know everybody else. Many performed Welsh folk dances to be overtaken by the loud beat of rock music. The feverish rhythm lasted a long time before fading into a slower tempo. By that time, he had consumed a couple of pints of beer while she was still on her first sherry. He took her in his arms for a dance. She pushed herself slightly against him. He felt her bosom. His heart beat faster. He felt blood rushing to every part of his body. His right hand dropped to hug her waist as they both lowered their clutched hands. Their cheeks were touching, and he was physically excited. The alcohol helped him overcome his inhibitions. He was blushing more than ever. He was worried that she may have felt his excited organ. If she did, she did not show it. Instead, she pushed herself in farther. He wanted her and wanted her badly. But due to their upbringing, there was only one way that could be achieved.

"Lesley, do you think … I mean … Would you consider …How shall I put it? … Will you marry me?"

"Yes, Arthur, I will!" She gave him a noisy kiss on the cheek and dragged him to a corner looking radiant and happy. "I thought you'd never ask."

"Maybe I shouldn't have. You know, it'll be several years before I start earn—"

"Hush." She put her hand on his mouth. "I'll be working. We'll manage."

"My mother said we could live with her."

"Splendid! But does she know? Did you tell her you were going to propose to me?"

"No, but she said she'd be very happy if you became my wife."

"Oh! I'm so happy! I can hardly wait to tell my parents and friends. I love this song. Let's dance, Arthur."

She hugged him tighter. He was her man—all of him with his wavy black hair, black eyes, slender but muscular figure, and rough hands. True, he was not too talkative—rather bashful—but he had a heart of gold. He would certainly make a fine husband and lover too. She could hardly wait for their life together to begin.

The wedding took place six months later. He remembered their wedding night in a hotel room in Ireland. Neither of them had had any previous sex experience. They were both shy. She could not get herself to undress in front of him. She slipped into the bathroom and emerged in a white nightgown. He had in the meantime gotten into his pajamas. They lay in bed and kissed. He lay on top of her, and his hand slipped in to feel her ample breasts. They were excited but too shy to get themselves to undress fully. She guided him into her, and when she screamed with pain, he pulled away in horror and confusion. The purported joys of sex were decidedly not apparent that first night, but in time, things improved on that front. A year later, Lesley gave birth to Janet, and Mary was born two years after that.

When Arthur finished his studies, he got in touch with his former principal and was over the moon with joy when he was offered a job as an instructor at his previous trade school. The principal had told him that they needed fresh blood to revise and update the curricula given the advances in technology, and since a couple of instructors were retiring, he was replacing them with young, more up-to-date instructors.

His mother was still working but was also happily busy with her grandchildren. With Lesley's salary and his, they managed to do a few things to change the drab appearance of the house. They introduced central heating, made changes in the bathroom and kitchen, and bought a few appliances. Life then seemed to settle into a routine. After exchanging a few words about the day's events, he would sit and read his newspaper and she would attend to the children and to chores. After dinner, they watched television before retiring.

This placid and tranquil life was marred only by his mother's death following a long illness four years after their marriage. The same routine was shattered a second time when one Sunday, Fr. Timothy asked to talk to them after the service.

"A few days ago, I received a letter from Fr. Ramos from the Philippines," Fr. Timothy had said. "I met him last year at a convention, and we hit it off very well. He believes the church should do more to help the poor and the dispossessed particularly in the developing world. As he put it, the church should not only concentrate on saving the souls but also on nourishing the bodies that sustain these souls. Quite an expansion of the dogma, I say.

"He's started a project. Youth from his church have been assisting homeless children, collecting them from the streets of Manila, giving them adequate shelter and education including religious education, introducing them to some sports, and basically assisting them to stand on their own feet. When we met, he mentioned that sixty youngsters were enrolled in that program, which was totally supported by voluntary contributions.

"He wrote me that he has set his eyes on the rural areas where the majority of the poor live. He wants to provide some of them with the means to increase their income beyond the subsistence level. He figures that many could do so by learning simple trades needed in rural areas—how to fix a bicycle, how to repair water pipes or taps, and so on. He's raised sufficient funds to start a project in some island in southern Philippines."

He picked up the letter and ran his finger over it. "Yes here it is. It's called Mindanao. He's been in touch with a British charitable organization. They're willing to provide what he called a mobile training unit, whatever that is, provided he presented them with the name and background information of a responsible person capable of managing the training unit and paying that person's salary and expenses. Fr. Ramos wrote that he's raised funds to cover a person's salary for two years initially apart from his travel expenses from England to Mindanao. He wondered if I could recommend a committed and dedicated person for this job. I thought I'd ask you if you'd be interested in taking on that assignment."

"Me?" exclaimed Arthur taken by surprise.

"Before making up your mind one way or the other, you and Lesley have to ponder two or three issues. First, your salary would not be much higher than what you're now earning, but I'm told the cost of living in the Philippines is almost half of what it is here or even less. Second, they'll be able to provide travel expenses only for you. This means you have to part with your family for a good two years or pay their travel costs yourself. But even assuming you were able to do so, where would you find schooling in a rural area overseas for your girls? Finally, you have to decide whether you would enjoy fieldwork where you may have to improvise in many cases as compared to a classroom situation with which you're familiar. I want you both to give this proposal careful thought and let me know in a week's time."

They walked out of the office in a daze.

Lesley was the first to speak. "I think you should go. We can use the money. Besides, Fr. Ramos is right. The church should be doing more than preaching the gospel. If you can be part of that endeavor, why not? Go for it! This is exciting, Arthur dear. And I know what's on your mind. Time will pass quickly. Two years isn't that bad. We'll manage as we always have."

After debating the issue for three more days, he told Timothy that he was prepared to go. He took two years' leave of absence from his school, but five months passed before the final approval came from Manila, and it took another month for his travel plans to be fixed.

So he was on his way—his first experience overseas. *What does the future hold for me?* He began to ponder the problems he was likely to face. It was not so much the professional aspects of the job; he felt confident on that score, *But what about the living conditions? Will the people accept me? Will I fit into this society so different from mine?*

The Rubys of Manila

After an hour stopover in Hong Kong and two more hours flying, Arthur made it to Manila. It was late September. The rainy season was almost over in that part of the world. He had been told that he would be met at the airport. He was wearing a tweed jacket and a tie. As he left the aircraft, the hot, humid air and the bright sunlight took him by surprise. Within minutes, he was sweating profusely.

Several other flights had recently arrived, so there were long lines at immigration and customs; it took him a good hour to clear them both. When he stepped out dragging his luggage, he found himself facing hundreds of people of all ages. Some were shouting and waving, some were crying, and others were laughing. The chaotic commotion was unsettling. Many people were holding signs with names on them, and he searched them for his name. A number of people offered to carry his luggage, to get him a taxi and a hotel room, to change currency, and so on. He finally spotted someone in his early twenties wearing a sport shirt and holding a sign bearing his name.

"Welcome to Manila, sir. My name is Rony. Hope you had a nice flight," he said with a broad grin. "You must be tired. It is a long flight I gather. I'll take you to your hotel to rest." He glanced at his watch. "It's three fifteen. We'll get there by four. You'll have a nice rest tonight, and I'll pick you up at ten thirty tomorrow morning. Fr. Ramos will receive you at eleven."

"When will I go to Mindanao?" Arthur asked.

"I suspect in three days, sir, but Fr. Ramos will give you all the details. You should enjoy Manila in the meantime. It's a great city."

Rory loaded Arthur's luggage into a taxi, and they climbed in. Noting Arthur's discomfort, Rony said with a broad smile, "You won't be needing a tie and a jacket in Mindanao. I hope you brought sport shirts."

"As a matter of fact I didn't, or at least not enough," Arthur said with some embarrassment. "I suspected it would be hot but not this hot."

"No problem. I'll take you shopping to a friend of mine. He will give you a discount. Anything you need, tell me. I have lots of friends here. They'll all give you a special price."

The printed smile returned to Rony's face. By then, the taxi was driving by the seaside. A strange smell of salt water and must filled the air. Many tall buildings and hotels lined the avenue some of them with a grayish-green moss covering parts of the façades. Hundreds of cars were competing with their taxi as their driver negotiated his way avoiding some potholes and other vehicles. Arthur was fascinated by the tricycle taxis all brightly colored and decorated with all sorts of shining metal artifacts.

After checking in at the hotel, he climbed a flight of stairs to his room. It was small and had just the bare necessities, but it had a bathroom and shower and was clean. Arthur heard street noise over that of the loud air conditioner. He collapsed in bed, but jet lag and the excitement brought on by this new environment deprived him of a deep sleep.

He was up and about several times during the night as he kept turning the air conditioning on and off. When he turned it off, he perspired profusely, and when he had it on, the humming noise was deafening.

He turned his thoughts to his scheduled meeting the following day. *What sort of details is Fr. Ramos likely to give me? What should I ask him?* The whole exercise was funded by contributions, and Arthur felt a responsibility to those who had donated. *Will I make a success of this assignment and live up to their expectations?* For hours on end, he tried to temper his anxiety and seek sleep but to no avail. It was not until four in the morning that he finally fell into a deep sleep only to be awoken four hours later by his alarm clock. *No morning tea here*, he thought as he showered, got dressed, and went down for breakfast—fresh papaya, which he tasted for the first time and liked, a bun, butter and jam, and tea, which he opted for instead of coffee. Rony showed up on time, and they were soon on their way to the parish.

He received a warm welcome from Fr. Ramos, who clasped his hand covering it with his other hand. "Welcome to Manila. I'm so pleased you came."

Ramos looked very different from what Arthur had expected. A man in his late forties, he was dressed in a casual sports shirt and blue jeans and had a wooden cross hanging on his chest. He was open and gregarious and invariably ended each sentence with a broad grin or a laugh, a person who was accustomed to and enjoyed an audience.

"I hope that your stay in our country will be pleasant despite your separation from your family. You'll have two more days here in Manila before your departure to Mindanao. This is not enough time for you to see such a big metropolis like Manila, but other opportunities will arise, I am sure, when you can come and spend a longer time here.

"On the other hand, you are going to a very beautiful island with very friendly people. Mindanao is rich in every respect. It has mineral resources, industries, and resort areas though with its fertile soil, agriculture constitutes the major activity of the population. Some parts of the island such as the city of Davao are highly industrialized. Other parts with their beautiful, white, sandy beaches adjacent to lush, green mountains have been developed as luxury resorts. The economic development of Mindanao, however, has been very uneven, and this is my and other people's concern, for among the fifteen or so provinces on the island, several are still backward and poverty stricken.

"I'm starting this project because I feel that the church should do something to alleviate poverty, give human beings a dignity that allows them to overcome their constant preoccupation with simply surviving so that they'll have time to nourish their souls. I hope you're free to join me for lunch."

Arthur nodded approval while thanking him.

Ramos continued. "We have high hopes for this project. Actually, here, most people go through basic education. The level of literacy is high in this country, but then, many people appear to be lost. Many cannot afford to further their education on one hand and are unable to find and hold onto regular jobs on the other. They find it difficult to bridge the gap between basic education and making a living. This situation is particularly acute in rural areas, where most of our poor people live.

"For a while now, I've been thinking of this problem. I sincerely believe that every problem creates an opportunity. If only these people are given a chance to be trained in simple basic trades, they can certainly generate some income and improve their lot in life. One can think of trades such as repairing a bicycle, a water pump, welding and pipe fitting for irrigation. One can also envisage more advanced training such as fixing cars, scooters, and even trucks or repairing radios and TV.

"The government has some technical schools and vocational training centers, but they're in the bigger cities on the island, out of reach of the average rural person. I am not a specialist in these fields, but I am convinced that the ideas are sound. They require a person like you to put them into practice. You need to decide on the type of training that enables trainees to apply it in a gainful manner. Nothing theoretical or too long—short, practical, and readily applicable."

Arthur was fascinated by what he heard. *What a challenge this latitude of choice is, and what a wonderful opportunity this is.*

Ramos continued. "I selected Mindanao not only because it is a rather large and mainly rural island with a few major towns but for other reasons as well. The population of twenty million are mainly Catholics. In fact, Catholics account for about seventy percent of the population with the remaining thirty percent being Muslims. For centuries, Catholics and Muslims lived side by side in perfect harmony. However, in the last two decades, a fundamentalist Islamic movement began to make its presence felt in Mindanao and particularly in its southern part. They capitalized on the prevailing poverty to attack the government accusing it of corruption and of neglecting the basic needs of the population.

"The movement itself is split into three major factions. A leader of one, Abu Sayyaf, has emerged in the last few years as one of the most determined and violent leaders. The Abu Sayyaf group probably numbers in the hundreds or maybe a couple of thousand, no more. Its members believe that more social justice will be attained by establishing an Islamic state in a stretch of islands that also include southern Mindanao. They feel overwhelmed by what they see as creeping Christian domination of what they consider rightly or wrongly their ancestral land. To that end, they have taken to armed struggle to further their cause.

"Ambushes of police stations and army patrols and the blowing up of pylons of power lines take place every once in a while. Don't be alarmed. They operate mainly in the south as I said, far from where we want you to be active initially. In consultation with the governor, I selected the city of Prosperidad for you to set base at the outset, and it's in the northern part of the island. What we would like you to do is to enroll Muslims and Catholics alike in your training courses. I believe we should restore harmony rather than amplify the schisms that our enemies are trying to promote. Who knows? Maybe through your work, some may want to join our church." Ramos smiled broadly. "Do you have any questions?"

"Yes. Several. How do I start? Where do I find the trainees? Do they speak English?"

"I alerted the Mindanao governor a few months ago about this project. He was very supportive and suggested the districts where you could operate. Following a further request from me, he notified some village heads asking them to publicize the idea among their populations. I suggest that

47

Rony accompanies you and stays with you in Prosperidad for six months. From this town, you could visit nearby villages. Rony will introduce you to the village heads and act as your interpreter and tutor, for I hope you can devote two hours a day to learning Tagalog, the national language. I suspect most people and especially townspeople will speak English, but in villages, some may or may not, and if you use difficult technical terms, many won't understand you.

"Your job is really to show and tell in a simple and comprehensive manner how to develop a certain skill, and I put the emphasis on the *show*. If you need advice or assistance, you can go to the local priest, but you report only to me."

They heard a knock at the door. A houseboy politely announced that lunch was ready.

"Come," said Ramos. "Let's have something to eat. In your honor, I will open a special bottle of wine I've been saving for this occasion." He walked to a cupboard and produced a bottle of white California chardonnay, pointed to the label, and said with a laugh, "As you can see, we all work for the grace of God." The producer's name, Christian Brothers, was written on the bottle in bold letters.

Rony, who attended the meeting, had sat respectfully silent throughout. He joined them for a meal of *bola-bola*— spicy but tasty fried fish balls—and rice. They had bananas and *rabutan* fruit for dessert. It was Arthur's second encounter with a tropical fruit, and he liked it too.

Over lunch, he learned that the mobile training unit had already arrived on the island. He and Ramos exchanged several ideas about project implementation, and when he rose to leave, Ramos handed him an envelope; it contained a ticket for his internal flight and an advance to help him get started. With that, Arthur bid Ramos farewell promising his best efforts to make a success of this project.

Rony suggested they go downtown so that he could show Arthur some of Manila's features. The hustle and bustle of the city was overwhelming. Thousands of people milled in the Makati downtown area. After an hour of walking and window-shopping, Rony looked up. Blue skies had now given way to threatening clouds. "It's the end of the rainy season. We'd better catch a taxi. Where do you want to go?"

"I'd better head to my hotel. I want to write to my wife and tell her I arrived safely. Besides I'm still jet-lagged."

"Fine. I'll come by to take you shopping tomorrow morning at nine. That will be our last day before we head to Mindanao."

They hardly made it to the hotel before the skies opened up with sheets of rain.

They spent the following day sightseeing and shopping. There was no shortage of tall, impressive buildings and shopping centers. Rony, ever proud of his city, showed him a nice suburb where the well-off lived and where several beautiful villas and homes were surrounded by a fence with armed guards at the entrance to the compound.

Other parts of the city consisted of more-modest buildings and apartment blocks while shantytowns could be seen far at the fringes of the city. Arthur realized that many of the clothes he had brought were unsuitable for the hot and humid tropical weather. Leather boots, woolen pants, ties, and long-sleeved shirts had to make way for sandals, tennis shoes, light cotton and polyester pants, and lots of short-sleeved sports shirts. Luckily, these items were either readily available to fit him or could be adjusted in a matter of hours.

He could not get over how cheap things were compared to back home. He was amused to see Rony arguing nicely with his friends over the price in every shop they went to. A first for him, an induction into the art of bargaining.

It was close to six in the evening. They had finished their chores. Rony said, "Now that we're done, we deserve a St. Miguel." Noting the incomprehension on Arthur's face, he continued with a broad grin. "I'm referring to our famous Filipino beer." He ushered Arthur into a dimly lit bar. Dense cigarette smoke hung in the air. A few modest wooden tables were scattered around. Several posters depicting love and sexy scenes, some originating probably from old movies or pageant shows, covered part of the walls. At the bar, which occupied a substantial area, two girls sat smoking. Rony arranged a couple of chairs around a table, went to the bar, and returned with a couple of bottles of St. Miguel beer. They had hardly sat down when one of the two girls at the bar came over, pulled a chair out, and sat close to Arthur. She waved to the waiter, who brought her a brandy.

"Hi! You American?"

"No, British."

"I love British people. They are so nice."

Arthur looked at her. She was barely twenty; she was slim with long, black hair and dark eyes, and she was wearing the tightest and shortest miniskirt he had ever seen—not that he had seen many. She wore a low-cut blouse that showed off her cleavage.

"My name's Ruby. What's yours?"

"He's Rony, and I'm Arthur."

"Arthur! That's my favorite name."

She pushed her chair closer to him. Her bare thigh was

touching his. He looked at her breasts and blushed. He was aroused and felt embarrassed. Rony was watching this scene with amusement. Arthur thought he noticed a mischievous look on Rony's face.

"Tell me, Arthur, do you like Filipina girls?" Ruby asked.

"Yes … Well …" He stumbled for words. "They're nice and friendly."

"They're sexy, and they become even sexier when they meet an attractive man like you," she said with a laugh. She bent over and blew into his ear. His blushing was beyond control. Apart from his wife, no woman had ever called him attractive or sexy. He felt elated. His desire for her grew by the minute.

"You're naughty, Arthur. I caught you looking at my breasts. Do you want to see them?" she asked with a teasing laugh. "Do you want the whole show? I think I know what you're after. I'll tell you in your ear. I don't want Rony to hear." She whispered, "You want to fuck me."

Arthur had never heard any woman use that word. *Is she really willing to have sex with me?* He was perspiring and at a loss for words while Rony was grinning broadly; he enjoyed watching foreigners succumb to the realities of life in Manila. To him, Arthur seemed a naïve, straight Westerner. What could be more interesting than to test this good married Catholic by putting him under the spell of a local bar girl?

"You know, Arthur, I'm so attracted to you that I'll make love with you for nothing. You only have to pay 200 pesos for the room."

Her right hand was gently caressing his thigh while she raised her left hand in a sign to the waiter to bring her another drink. Arthur was bursting with desire, but before he knew it, Rony gulped his beer down, stood, grabbed Arthur by the hand, and waved the waiter off.

"Where are you going? Wait a minute!"

"Sorry, Ruby," Rony interjected. "We have to go to an important appointment. We'll come back tonight around eight. Will you be here?" Without waiting for an answer, he guided Arthur out of the bar. When Arthur got up, he felt exposed and thought everyone must have noticed his physical excitement. He was embarrassed. It took a few minutes of walking in the street before he felt the pain of cooling off.

Arthur asked, "Are we going back to that bar tonight?"

"Of course not. You don't have to mean everything you say."

"She's a nice girl, Ruby."

"You like her, you can go back if you wish. She'll take 170 pesos from you for her lovemaking and pay 30 pesos for the room. That's how it works."

"I can't get over her drinking brandy in this heat."

"What brandy? The only similarity her drink has to brandy is its price. This was tea served in a brandy glass. There are thousands of Rubys in Manila. They come from rural areas, broken homes. They're like butterflies attracted to city lights and end up being burned by them."

Arthur was startled. All Ruby had said about his sex appeal had been a game, one he had never played before. He could not help feeling how exciting it was though. He could probably have played a similar game in London or some other city back home, but he had never tried. *Have I missed something in life?*

On Assignment

The two-hour flight to Mindanao was uneventful, but as the plane made its final approach, Arthur was overcome by the beauty of the land below—lush, green vegetation, banana and coconut trees, some thatched-roof houses, and rice paddies interspersed with ponds of water.

As he stepped off the plane, he again got a whiff of the hot, steamy weather. It was definitely hotter than Manila he thought, but he was better prepared for it. His tweed jacket, wool pants, and tie had been replaced by a sports shirt and light cotton pants. A cap and a pair of sunglasses shielded him from the bright sunlight.

After collecting their belongings, Arthur and Rony climbed in a taxi for the drive to their destination—the city of Prosperidad, which lay on the main road linking Davao, the capital of Mindanao, to the northern tip of the island. Temporary accommodation had been secured from Manila by phone at a local hotel. As they approached the city center, the taxi driver had to maneuver his way through a maze of vehicles of all sorts—cars, vans, bicycles, tricycles, motorcycles, scooters, trucks, and even the occasional oxcart. Some were belching black fumes while others tooted their horns in a disjointed chorus. Several young men and boys crisscrossed the traffic to sell newspapers, nuts, cigarettes, and packs of tissue paper, and others offered to clean windshields at traffic lights. They all seemed to be struggling to eke out a living.

On the sidewalks, people walked slowly in the tropical heat past shops selling everything from coconuts to vegetables, fish, spices, shoes, sandals, and sarongs. There were also cafés and makeshift eating counters and restaurants, some frying fish or bananas in plain view of passers-by hoping the sight or the smell would entice them in.

Arthur kept a curious look at his surroundings. He had seen similar scenes on television in Wales, but he was no longer an observer; he was about to become part of a new culture. Exciting as that was, he could not help making a comparison with his hometown. True, this was a noisy place, and some of the eating places did not look all that clean, but it was alive. There were no inhibitions, no closed doors hiding merchandise, no particular effort to protect passers-by from the occasional stands or chairs on the pavement, no particular dress code. It was all out in the open for everyone to see and watch. He took a deep breath of the humid tropical air and felt more relaxed.

The modest hotel room was clean and adequate. No air conditioning; instead, an electric fan adorned the ceiling. Rony advised him to keep it on as it fulfilled two functions— swirling cooler air around and chasing mosquitos away. Their stay in that hotel lasted a week before Rony managed to find a small, sparsely furnished apartment to rent.

Six weeks passed before Arthur ran his first training course in pipe fitting, welding, and water pump maintenance and repair. The course was held in a schoolyard in a nearby village. He had spent time visiting some villages' elderly, talking through Rony to prospective trainees, receiving and getting acquainted with the mobile training unit, and preparing simple course material with plenty of exercises. He decided to start with three villages conducting the pipe-fitting course in one village, a course in household electric extensions and repairs in a second village, and a course on car engine repairs in the third village. These courses were to be run one after the other and publicized in the three villages as well as other villages. He felt like a one-man band or a jack-of-all-trades, but his was basic, rudimentary training delivered in a simple manner intended for simple people.

Some fifteen people showed up for his first course. Their number dwindled to ten by the time the course was over, but by then, they were a happy group of ten. He was deeply moved when on the last day several showed up with presents—a bunch of bananas, some coconuts, a few fresh eggs, mangos, dried flowers … They all thanked him profusely, and he felt elated and fulfilled. He enjoy a sense of achievement he had rarely felt before.

He wrote his first report to Ramos. Among other things, it had slipped his mind in Manila to ask for funds to buy materials for training such as piping, electric wiring and switches, and soldering material. He reckoned he would need 1,500 pesos, roughly $100, over the next six months for that. He had written earlier, and Ramos had sent him 800 pesos promising to send the rest in due course.

As he wrote, he had to explain his predicament. He needed to buy rather urgently a used car the trainees could use to learn basic automotive maintenance. He had shopped around with Rony but could find nothing for less than 8,000 pesos, and that was for an old car that was not in a good working order but would do for training. His mobile training unit contained a cross section of a car engine that would help explain how the engine worked, but he wanted his trainees to put their hands in the dirt and get the feel for the nuts and bolts of it all.

He was anxious because his intended course in car engine repairs was so popular and oversubscribed that he had decided to hold it twice. It was three weeks before the answer came back. Ramos had enclosed a check for 2,000 pesos explaining that it was the best he could do for the moment. He suggested that Arthur buy a used engine rather than a whole car.

For two days, Arthur pondered the issue, and then, he hit on a brilliant idea. His trainees were a mixed bag. Several were already in the car repair business. They had learned their profession watching others or by their own wits. They felt that if they attended his course, they might learn a trick or two to add to their bag of tricks. Others were young aspiring mechanics who felt they could probably be able to borrow money from family and friends to start a small garage somewhere. *Why not ask those who are interested to bring in the cars of their clients to the classroom?* Arthur thought. He would assist his trainees in diagnosing the problem, put them on to fix the engine under his guidance, and would charge 250 pesos from the trainee and garage owner per car plus any materials or lubricants needed. The trainee could then charge his client as he saw fit making his profit without even working on the car except as a trainee like all the others. If four cars were brought in for maintenance or repairs, he could collect a thousand pesos for his petty cash to buy material for his training.

Rony thought it was a brilliant idea, but he cautioned Arthur about revealing this scheme to Ramos. "Before you know it," he said, "they'll want an account of your petty cash. Besides, this is not a guaranteed income. Maybe one time you'll have four cars and another time you'll have none. What about the eight-thousand-peso car you saw? You won't need it any more in this case."

"I've been thinking about it. It needs a lot of fixing. I'm thinking of buying it myself. Perhaps the trainees can strip its engine as an exercise."

It was a ten-year-old Toyota. As the owner put it, he had become fed up with repeated repairs by incompetent mechanics and was finally in a position to afford a better secondhand car. The chassis was in a reasonable shape with a dent on the back fender. The tires were threadbare, the interior had a faded color of blue with seat springs that had lost their bounce and plastic covering that was cracked in places. One of the side windows was stuck and would not go up or down. The windshield wipers worked, but the rubber had cracked on one and was almost gone from the other.

Arthur figured out that with a complete overhaul, the car could be substantially improved and could even fit his need for a personal car. With help from Rony, he managed to bring the price down to 7,000 pesos promising ready cash. The Toyota had 87,000 kilometers on it, not that much, Arthur thought, but most of those kilometers had been acquired through city and dirt-road driving, and that had taken its toll on the car. He could afford it. Part of his salary was paid in pesos and the rest in US dollars. He had been transferring most of his dollars to Wales. In addition, over the past three months he had accumulated quite a lot of pesos and had no time to inquire on how best to transfer a good part of these as well. The procedure for currency transfer was complicated he was told despite the fact that the peso itself was readily transferable to dollars and vice versa if it was in cash.

His electricity course was another success. He had twenty trainees; only two dropped out. They practiced laying and joining wires and switches on planks of wood. There was a great deal of enthusiasm when he managed to convince two rural entrepreneurs to let his trainees help them with the electric work on their building sites all to be done under his and the entrepreneurs' close supervision.

He was again showered with presents, but that time, he had tears in his eyes when two trainees presented him with a wooden cross engraved with mother of pearl. He was deeply moved because these two trainees were Muslims. All his life, he had been brought up to shun other religions and even to differentiate himself from other denominations in the Christian faith. With the cross, he was handed a reminder that barriers between religions erected by human beings could easily be lowered by simple gestures from other human beings. He had to travel halfway around the world to learn that.

Man is a differentiating animal, he thought. *Everyone's constantly striving to find something that makes him different from others—nationality, religion, race, educational level, social status, places of birth, on and on.* All these factors certainly applied in his case. He was markedly different from his trainees on every one of those counts, but his ardent desire was to be accepted as one of them. He wanted to obliterate rather than magnify the barriers that made him stand out.

These thoughts crossed his mind on several occasions when at times he lay awake at night. He felt a sense of accomplishment with what he was doing as he could see the fruit of his work. Ramos had in fact written to comment on one of his reports and suggested it might be a good idea for him to make the rounds of his graduate trainees two or three months later and find out how many were using the training and generating some income. Ramos wanted facts and figures to satisfy himself and his financial backers as to the soundness of their donations.

Arthur thought that was a good idea. He postponed the date he had set for his third course and set about with Rony to visit his former trainees in the various surrounding villages. He was happy to report back that in almost 70 percent of the cases, his former students were selling their services part time with a noticeable increase in their income. There were even two cases of trainees who had set up businesses and were busy about 40 to 50 percent of the time. In 20 percent of the cases, the trainees used the skills acquired for their own purposes such as maintaining and repairing their own pumps instead of waiting days and paying others to do so. A few said that while they had learned a lot that was interesting, they had no time to apply it and had drifted back to their old occupations.

Four months had passed since his arrival on the island, and he was ready for his course on car maintenance and repairs, which was oversubscribed. He was counting on this course to fill his petty cash fund. At first, he explained to his trainees how car engines worked showing models and drawings from his mobile training unit. Then he invited his class to work on the engine of his car. They were able to lift it out, put it on a bench, and disassemble it. He did not ask them to put it back together; he planned on doing that himself after a thorough cleaning and inspection.

He then presented his idea of inviting them to bring in their clients' cars. To his surprise, eight cars were brought in the following day. Like a doctor in a hospital, he moved around from one car to another with his trainees showing them how to diagnose each car's problems. Then he divided his twenty-five trainees into groups, each group working on one car under his supervision.

He collected 2,000 pesos for this service and added them to the 2,000 pesos Ramos had sent. His petty cash was overflowing. His trainees asked him to teach them how to repair motorbike engines, and he said he would if they provided the bikes. Repair fees were 100 pesos per motorbike. Three motorcycles and two scooters were brought in, and he became 500 pesos richer. After another repetition of the course and another 2,000 pesos earned, the time had come for him to move to new pastures.

Ramos had explained in Manila that in agreement with the governor, Arthur was expected to extend his activities to three other locations in Mindanao. As a result, he moved to the next assigned provincial town, Marawi. Some hundred thousand souls lived in that city, which lay at the northern tip of a large lake on the island. It was to be his base for the next six months. From there, he would go to nearby villages to run his courses repeating the pattern he had done earlier. Rony, whose six months were coming to an end, joined him at Marawi. He introduced him to the city and village elders and helped him launch his activities in that new environment.

Arthur regretted Rony's imminent departure very

much. They had hit it off well. Rony had been a great pillar of strength especially in those early days when everything was new to Arthur. He explained to him the customs and habits of the village people, answered many of his queries, introduced him to local food and drink, and was his unfailing interpreter. His biggest contribution, however, was as a language teacher. They spent two hours each day and sometimes more working on Arthur's Tagalog. Rony worked hard on Arthur's pronunciation in particular.

He also encouraged him to use the limited vocabulary he had when conducting his second array of training courses. "It's better to teach using sign language and the few words you know than straight English with an interpreter. That way, you'll pick up more of the language and identify more with your trainees." he told him.

Above all, Arthur appreciated his courteous, self-effacing personality and his ever-present smile. To celebrate Rony's departure, he invited him for dinner at one of the better restaurants in town. They had prawns, seafood, and fish with rice and washed them down with bottles of St. Miguel. During the meal, they reminisced about various incidents, some funny, others less so, and talked about Ruby. Rony was candid. "You really went for that girl. I mean Ruby."

"I didn't know she was a prostitute. To tell you the truth, I hadn't met one before coming here."

"Well, Arthur, you'll be staying here for another year and a half or so. You mean to tell me you won't sleep with a woman here?"

"I'm a married man!"

"Bullshit! If the women in this country slept only with single men, half the prostitutes would be out of business in no time. Many married men have girlfriends or mistresses. Most of our politicians and high-ranking officials are known to have affairs, and that doesn't raise an eyebrow. People take these happenings in stride. Why make a fuss over a love or a sex affair? If anything, lovers should be envied. There is a love of life in the Philippines. President Marcos came from the military, yet he and his wife sang in public on many occasions. Everybody loves partying, singing, dancing, and really enjoying life."

"But I thought the majority were Catholics and didn't deviate readily from the teachings of the church."

"Sure, but only on Sundays. On Sundays, they go to church and take communion, but they succumb to their desires the other days of the week. To them, religion and enjoyment are not mutually exclusive. It is natural to love and make love most people feel. If an opportunity arises and a man and a woman want each other, why should they abstain and go against nature?"

When the two were saying their goodbyes the following day, they shook hands and then hugged. Arthur felt lonely and alone that day. Their discussion the previous night haunted him. He kept turning Rony's words in his mind: "You mean to tell me you won't sleep with a woman here?" "It is natural to love and make love most people feel. If an opportunity arises, why should one go against nature?" He wondered how he would behave if an opportunity came his way. The more he thought about it, the less sure he became of finding the right answer.

The short rainy season had come and gone, and at the beginning of April, he started his activities in the villages surrounding Marawi. At times, he wished he was more versatile or that he had professional help; several people had asked him if he could train them in radio and TV repair, woodworking and cabinet making, masonry … The needs were insatiable, but he had no proficiency in those fields.

On one sunny and unusually warm afternoon, he went to a shop in town to buy mosquito repellent. Finding none on the shelf, he headed to the cash counter to inquire. A woman was there paying for her purchases. When she heard him raise the question, she readily said, "I'm afraid I took the last one." The shopkeeper told him that he would have the repellent the following day; if he needed it right away, there was a shop a five-minute walk away he could try. Noting his hesitancy about directions, the woman volunteered to show him the way. "I'm walking that way anyway. My name's Sonya."

He introduced himself, and the two set off on what turned out to be closer to a fifteen-minute walk. She was in her early thirties and attractive, well dressed and groomed, and had a polished manner of speaking. She figured out that he was British from his accent and wondered what he was doing in Marawi. He began to tell her about his work. She listened and found it interesting bordering on the fascinating. As they passed a candy shop, she gently interrupted him.

"I must step in here for a second. I promised my children I'd buy them some candy. I have two, a girl, six, and a boy, five. And you?"

He told her about his two girls and Lesley. Without sadness or bitterness, she casually mentioned that she was separated from her husband.

When they got to the other shop, he bought the mosquito repellent, but then he noticed a coffee and a juice place next door and asked if he could offer her a cold drink. She readily accepted.

"That'll give me a chance to hear more about your experiences in our country." She sat lifting one leg over the other, her pink dress receding slightly above her knee. He could not help looking at her legs and imagining the rest of her body. A faint smell of perfume attracted him to her further. He wished he could bury his head against her slender neck and get a good whiff. He watched her slightly uplifted nose, her thin lips, and her very slightly slanted black eyes with pronounced eyelashes. His shyness did not allow him more than a few seconds of probing at a time, but he felt he was uncontrollably falling under her spell.

He had in fact been attracted to several Filipina girls before. They were very different from the girls back home and not only physically; they were outgoing and less reserved, and they always put on attractive smiles and giggled. He had tried to justify this attraction by blaming it on the curiosity and excitement often associated with probing a partner whose background is very different. He was alone, and he longed particularly for female company. *Maybe I should overcome my inhibitions and ask her out? There should be no problem. I've always kept my desires and feelings at bay.*

Sonya appeared to come from a well-to-do background. She told him she had never been to England or Europe but had visited Singapore, Hong Kong, and the United States. She did want to get to Europe someday, and London and Paris were high on her list of priorities.

When she rose to leave, Arthur said he had enjoyed talking to her so much. "Can I see you again?" he asked in a bashful manner.

She hesitated but then said, "Don't tell me you want

to buy another can of spray." She giggled and added, "OK, why not?"

"Can you make it Sunday?"

"No, I devote Sunday to my children and my mother and visiting or receiving visits from other members of the family. Saturday would be OK."

"That's fine. Can we have lunch or dinner?"

"I prefer the evening, when it's cooler and all the chores of the day will have been done."

And so they parted only to meet three days later. He looked forward with great anticipation to seeing her again. She arrived wearing an elegant fitted turquoise-blue dress that skirted the top of her knee. He had selected a Chinese restaurant, and no sooner had they sat down to their meal than she asked him about life in England and Wales. She also wanted to know more about his family, and he obliged. He then asked her discreetly about her married life.

"We separated four years ago. We aren't divorced. Divorce is rather difficult in this country. He left me for another girl. Maybe I became less attractive after my second pregnancy. We'd fallen in love in our teens. We got married and were very happy ... At least I thought so. He's a very nice person— jovial, good looking, generous, and obliging. I suppose that makes him attractive to many women."

There was no bitterness in her voice. She seemed to be trying to justify her husband's behavior. He admired her.

"Let's change the subject," she said. "How about going to the movies tonight?"

"What's on?"

"Two of the latest action movies, one with Schwarzenegger and the other with Stallone. Hong Kong–produced movies in which people walk on walls, jump across roofs, and kill each other with the greatest of ease. Action movies are very popular here, and so are love movies and sagas. *Yanks* with Richard Geer is also showing, and there's one theater that shows old movies. I was looking at the papers today. Guess what's on? *Zorba the Greek*!"

"I never saw it."

"You haven't? You must see it. I saw it many years ago. It's about a Greek, Zorba, urging an Englishman to get over his inhibitions. I won't tell you anymore."

"Can we make it?"

She looked at her watch.

"If we skip dessert and leave right away, we probably won't miss more than the first five minutes. You see, Arthur, there's an advantage to being a single woman once again. I'm a free agent. I can return home anytime I want. I don't owe an explanation to anybody."

It was around midnight when he drove her home after watching the film. He told her how much he had enjoyed their evening. He had found the acting and the scenery in the film absolutely brilliant.

She did not need much persuasion to agree to another dinner with him a few days later. Once more, they had a lot to talk about. When dinner was over, Arthur suggested that they go for a walk in a park or some other place away from the cigarette smoke and noisy crowds. "But does a place like this exist?" he asked.

"Come on. I'll take you. There's a nice walk by the lake. I often take the children for evening walks there. It should be quiet at this late hour."

A short drive brought them to a paved pathway skirting the

lake where they saw brightly lit restaurants along the waterfront. The night air was cooler but smelled a bit musty. A few empty fishing boats lay about in the water moving up and down with the tiny waves. A light breeze caressed some palm and coconut trees on the side of the road, and they responded by swaying gently releasing a faint hissing sound. The moon wore one of its many faces—a silver crescent surrounded by hundreds of bright stars. Not many people crossed their way. It was not only the late hour, but as Sonya remarked, most people were glued to their television sets as an important football game was on that night. They crossed three or four lovers holding hands and whispering to each other with whom they exchanged faint smiles. Arthur and Sonya walked in silence as if afraid to disturb the serenity of nature. Arthur was the first to speak.

"I can't get over your husband. How can any man leave you? You're beautiful, Sonya."

"Beautiful not so much," she said with a smile. "Attractive yes."

She lent him her hand. He grasped it firmly. They walked in silence, and then she stopped and turned to him. She put her arms around him and brought her lips closer to his. They kissed; it was a long kiss with affection but no passion. They resumed walking.

"Arthur, I'd like to see where you live."

"It's a small, modest place, two rooms, really nothing much to see."

"Take me there."

They drove to his apartment. She looked around approvingly.

"Do you want something to drink?"

Sonya opened her arms. "I want a hug instead."

They kissed passionately again and again. She then liberated herself from his arms and unzipped her skirt. Before she could unhook it and let it slip down, he put his hand on hers and stopped her from doing so. "Sonya, I'd better drive you home." She looked at him in disbelief as if she had just been rudely awakened from a beautiful dream. She pulled herself together, and without a word, they left the apartment.

When they met three days later, they had little to say to each other; both felt embarrassed. She did not want a meal but accepted a drink in a coffee shop. He suggested they go for a walk to that path by the lake, but she turned him down. "I hope my behavior last time didn't offend you too much," she said in a rather sarcastic manner and with a touch of anger.

He fumbled for words. "No, no, heavens no. It's just that I'm a married man and—"

"Arthur, I think we should stop seeing each other. Things developed so fast. They always do in hot climates like ours compared to the colder climates in other countries," she said, again with a touch of sarcasm. "It's like they say—Quick to grow, quick to die. Goodbye, Arthur. I really enjoyed meeting you." She extended her hand to him.

"But why?"

"Arthur, it's goodbye."

"Let me drive you home."

"No thank you. I know my way."

When Arthur returned home that evening, he felt lonely and hollow and angry with himself. He was like a prisoner who could not break his chains, a prisoner of his own upbringing, traditions, and established values. He longed to be free, to live and love and act normally without inhibition, fear, or guilt. He had squandered an opportunity for no reason except his stupidity. Here was an attractive woman, a willing partner with no strings attached, and what did he do? He wanted to keep it platonic when she was offering him her body. What could she have possibly thought of him? An impotent person, an immature lover unsure of his sex drive, or a hopeless character to be pitied? If only she gave him another chance, he would prove her wrong.

If anything happened, Lesley did not have to know about it. It would have become his closely guarded secret, something to cherish and revisit whenever he felt the burden of a stale marriage or yearned for affection. What would it have been like to have sex with Sonya? A warm, affectionate, outgoing Filipina would probably have taught him a thing or two about lovemaking. She would have probably brought him untold contentment in bed. What a missed opportunity. If only he is given another chance, if only he knew where she lived, or how to contact her, but even then, would she be willing to overlook his odd behavior? Then he remembered Zorba: "There is one thing a woman can never forgive," Zorba had said in the movie in his broken English. "If she invites a man to her bed and he will not go."

Over the next few months, Sonya crossed his mind many times. He had to get over it. He immersed himself in his work and again felt that he was accomplishing a lot. By the end of his first year, 132 trainees had gone through his programs and over 100 were using what they had learned to augment their income. It was time once more to move on. Ramos had suggested villages near a third provincial town, the town of Kipagah in the southern part of the island. That town was close to where the troubles were; Abu Sayyaf and his group had made several forays into that district.

Didi

Arthur settled into a hotel room in his new environment, Kipagah, in the southeastern part of the island. It seemed to have sprung from nowhere. The surroundings were lush, green, and hilly. It was a good hour and a half drive or so to the coast on rural roads that were easier to negotiate during the dry season.

He went out to explore the city. He walked down several streets and alleys before coming to a square, which seemed to pool several of the city's functions. It was cobblestoned and had room for several shops and cafés and two restaurants. The square appeared to be the meeting place of choice for people there.

To get his bearings, he asked some people about the population of Kipagah. Someone told him it was forty thousand, another doubled that number, while a third person shrugged in indifference. Still, he enjoyed exploring the city before returning to his room almost an hour later sweating and feeling the heat. A cold shower cooled him off.

After chasing off a few mosquitoes, he sat in an armchair, poured a cold beer, and became pensive. He felt that he had already changed in many ways, for the better he reckoned. He certainly had been green when he first arrived in the country.

Perhaps his life in Wales was too placid, too steady, devoid of variety. It all went at a consistent and almost predictable rhythm; nothing out of the ordinary seemed to happen. By contrast, in the Philippines, life seemed to coast along without much planning and pondering; things were less regimented and at times bordering on the chaotic to a Westerner, but it was certainly exciting, and the unpredictable often happened.

Professionally, he also believed that he had perhaps accomplished more meaningful results in this country than he would have teaching regular students back home. His present work provided him with a great sense of satisfaction, and he felt confident of success in the remaining part of his assignment.

He was happy to have risen to the challenge of becoming an entrepreneur with his petty cash, which grew steadily with every car maintenance course he ran. It helped him purchase material for his training activities, pay for the gasoline of his mobile training unit, and organize graduation parties at the end of each course at which he served soft drinks and biscuits and handed each graduate an attendance certificate. These certificates were highly valued by his trainees. He saw nothing wrong in hiding the existence of his petty cash; it avoided his having to ask for handouts from Manila. He planned to turn over to Ramos whatever money was in the kitty when he left the country.

All along, he had been respected and liked by his trainees. He spoke reasonably well Tagalog though at times he had difficulty deciphering regional languages and dialects. Apart from the improved language ability, he had come to understand better the country's culture and the behavior of its people. He had long stopped comparing their attitudes to those of the people he knew back home accepting them as they were instead.

Still, work accomplishments apart, there was a sense of emptiness in his life. He longed for affection, love, sex. It was a constant struggle to keep a lid on his desires. He tried to fill this void partly by writing to Lesley. At first, he had written lengthy letters each week describing the country, his work, every aspect of his life, and anecdotes concerning his students or others he met. He described the food and fruit and what was available at the markets, the vegetation and flowers, the daily downpour during the rainy season when village children would happily play in the rain. But as time went by, he had fewer things to write about that he had not already covered. His writings slipped down to twice a month and sometimes even less.

Lesley wrote back about once a month. Her letters were shorter. She told him about their daughters, their schooling, any particular incidents that affected her work, and news about neighbors and friends.

Absent from their letters were passionate words of love. The cryptic usual endings were always there—"With much love" or "Missing you, take care"—but that was all. It was not enough to nourish the passion of a lonely man or for that matter a woman alone separated by thousands of miles.

He had other preoccupations. He wanted to select villages that were not in troubled areas. Apart from the city authorities, he would seek the advice of local priests. As in every city he had been to, there were several Catholic churches. He made some discreet inquiries and was directed to the St. Pedro Church whose priest, Fr. Angel, was known to be among the longest serving in the city and the wisest.

He decided he would speak to him after the church service on Sunday.

At church, he prayed in earnest and knelt as the priest blessed the host and wine. When it was time for communion, he moved from his seat to the central aisle to line up with others. On the other side, a girl dressed in white covering her hair with an embroidered white scarf also approached the line. With her droopy head and half-closed eyes, she looked stunning. He quickly made way for her and walked right behind her toward the altar. How absurd it was to feel attracted to a girl at this holiest moment of mass. He tried hard to dismiss this thought from his mind. He focused his sights and attention on the cross lying on the altar, on Fr. Angel trying to draw strength to chase any unwarranted feelings.

When the service was over, he slipped outside waiting to speak to Angel once he finished greeting the congregation. Still, he felt the urge of wanting to see that girl again. He saw her in a group of four men and two other girls. They were talking and giggling. She had taken off her scarf revealing dark hair groomed evenly to the bottom of her slender neck and curving slightly upward on one side. She had big, almond-shaped, black eyes, a tiny nose, and full lips. He could not help noticing her beautiful body, lovely legs, proportionately shaped hips, and bosom whose inviting contours were partly evident through her white silk blouse. With her high heels, he figured she was only a shade shorter than he was.

The more he looked at her, the more he wanted to look again. She must have been the most beautiful girl he had seen since coming to this country, even the most attractive girl he had ever seen. All the while, she never looked his way or acknowledged his presence. Soon, she and her companions left. The congregation bidding Angel goodbye dwindled to the stubborn few who were engaged in lengthy conversations. It was finally Arthur's turn to do so. He introduced himself to the willowy old priest and explained the advice he was seeking. Angel listened intently. He knew Ramos in Manila, whom he praised for the initiative that Arthur was undertaking.

"Unfortunately," Angel began, "incidents in this province can neither be predicted nor are they daily affairs. It is safe to say, however, that all villages within twenty kilometers from this town have always been peaceful. Beyond that radius, you would be moving into the unpredictable. Some villages only thirty kilometers away have been attacked while others fifty kilometers farther have been safe up till now. The poor villagers don't know where to turn. Sometimes, they're attacked by fanatics wanting to destabilize the government, and other times, by army patrols chasing real or imaginary rebels in their midst. Stay within twenty kilometers from here and you'll be reasonably safe. I cannot tell you any more, nor can I predict what can happen. I cannot play God."

Arthur expressed his appreciation for the advice. As he prepared to leave, Angel added, "This is a nice town. I hope you enjoy it. Where are you staying?"

"At a hotel at the moment. I'm trying to find a small furnished flat to settle in for the next several months. Do you, Father, by any chance know somebody from the congregation who has anything like that for rent?"

"Let me ask around. I hope I'll see you next Saturday at our evening."

"What evening?"

"Once a year, we organize a party to raise money for the church right here in the churchyard. We rent tables and chairs. We can seat two hundred here. Many people will be offering food, drinks, and desserts for sale. The organizing committee makes sure that the bar is well stocked and that there's plenty of food. A band usually plays, and there will be folk dances and normal dancing. Filipinos create any excuse to have a party, so why not? And it's the easiest way to raise contributions. Announce a party and it becomes a big success before it even starts!"

"I'll be very happy to come, Father."

"Good. I'll see you then."

They shook hands warmly before parting.

During the week, Arthur kept thinking about the nameless girl he had seen at church. He let his imagination carry him to a scenario in which he would be dating and falling in love and even having sex with her. His fantasy carried him further. He tried to imagine what lovemaking with her would be like. If only it happened, he was sure it would be passionate and lustful, a love to the finish, one that went on and on until one partner finished the other off. That much accomplished in theory, reality would then take over. He would remind himself that he was a married man with children and had a mission to fulfill; he would chide himself for allowing his dreams to carry him that far. At any rate, that girl would surely be at the church party; no harm done if the occasion presented itself for him to meet her.

On Saturday evening, he arrived at the church hall. A platform had been set up on one side. A hundred or so people had already scattered around many of the tables, and others were milling around. Some women and men stood behind food stands and a bar. He was sure that as the evening progressed, many more people would show up.

Colored light bulbs hung in rows on a wire and swayed with the wind. Loud recorded music blared interrupted once in a while by a person with a microphone urging people to buy lottery tickets. There were people of all ages including children. Everybody was dressed in his or her Sunday best. A clearing space was reserved in front of the platform for dancing, but it was too small a space to allow much movement if all two hundred or even a quarter of them decided to dance.

People kept coming in jockeying for tables and chairs. There were shouts of greetings across tables and loud laughter from various corners. With the music, the microphone announcements, and the crowds, Arthur felt the noise level was fast approaching the threshold of pain. He did not know anybody and walked between the tables and among the crowd looking for his nameless girl, but she was nowhere to be found. He then spotted Angel, the only person he knew, busy talking with two men. He waited patiently before going over to shake his hand.

"Oh! There you are. Come. There's someone I want you to meet. I think I may have found something for you."

Arthur did not comprehend what he was referring to, but he followed squeezing between tables, chairs, and people. Angel stopped by a table and told someone, "Miguel, meet …" He temporarily forgot Arthur's name.

"Arthur," Arthur interjected stretching his hand out.

"Miguel will tell you all about it."

Angel left them and hurried back to solve more problems with his fund-raising event.

"Are you alone?" Miguel asked. "Why don't you join us?"

Arthur accepted mixing his words of thanks with appreciation. There must have been more than a dozen around that table including four children. Introductions were made all around, but by the time they were over, he had forgotten who was who.

"Fr. Angel told me you were looking for a place to rent for a few months. No problem. We have an apartment for rent, but I don't know if it'll suit you. It's on the outskirts of town. I have a small garage where my younger brother, Ramon, and I keep busy. Our house is beside the garage, and a year or so ago, we added a second floor for a member of the family who was getting married, but that got put off, so the apartment's available. Are you married, Arthur?"

"Yes. I have two girls. My wife and the children are in England or I should say Wales. I'm alone here."

"But then the apartment may be too big for you."

"No, please. I'd love to see it if that's all right with you. How interesting that you have a garage."

"Cars have been my hobby ever since I was fourteen. I used to cut pictures of cars and scotch tape them on the walls in my room. All sorts of cars, old models, sport cars, fancy cars that appeared in movies like 007's Austin Martin and so on. Then one day, I guess I was sixteen at the time, I gave my father the biggest shock of his life. I brought home a big, twenty-year-old Thunderbird car. I'd bought it for a thousand pesos. I'd been pestering my mother for a couple of years to lend me money to buy a car, and she finally gave in.

"I had big dreams of painting the car red and driving it in town. No girl could resist it I thought." He laughed. "The only problem was that nothing in that car worked. I spent hours every day scraping the old paint and attempting to fix the engine, but I couldn't put it back together properly. I started asking other garage owners but got skimpy answers. Friends came to help, and Ramon joined in. That car became everything to me.

"I finally dropped out of school. I wasn't good at studies anyway. My father tried to reason with me but to no avail. He would ask me, 'How can you trade your education and your future for a car?' My mother was more realistic. She told me that maybe I'd make a profession of my hobby.

"Then the big day came. Among the cheers of neighbors and friends, I drove my red Thunderbird for thirty meters before it stalled and wouldn't start again. I started working on it again. That was ten years ago. In the meantime, my father died, heartbroken I am sure. I opened my garage urged by friends to do so. Ramon later joined me. That car taught me all I knew about car mechanics. Now I told you everything. How about you? What brings you to Mindanao and to Kipagah?"

Arthur explained briefly what he was doing and said he was hoping to start a course on automotive repairs in a couple of weeks.

"Count me in, and if you repeat it, Ramon will also join."

They were interrupted by an announcement urging people to get their food and drink for the show was about to begin. Several persons at their table made a move toward the food stands. Arthur offered to go, but they would not hear of it; he was their guest.

On the platform, some schoolchildren performed a short play to cheers and claps from proud parents, and a ten-year-old boy played the violin. Next, a choir sang a few Filipino folk songs. Some members of the crowd joined in, others listened intently, and a few women wiped tears from their eyes. Amid loud cheers, the choir left the stage to four young men dressed in the national costume holding four long, thick bamboo poles. They squatted on the floor. Two of them faced each other with each person holding in each hand the ends of the poles. The other two persons did the same thing right beside them.

"Our bamboo dance," whispered Miguel to Arthur, who was by that time spellbound—his dream girl had appeared on the stage. She was dressed in a Filipino national dress, cream in color with exaggerated, starched, lifted, and almost flat short sleeves. With a serene look on her face, she was well groomed and barefoot. Then the dance began. The two men opposing each other, with each holding the thick bamboo pole, banged the thick poles on the floor, lifted them up slightly, and then banged them together with force and a clicking rhythm. The two persons beside them repeated the same motion starting a few seconds later. Then the dancer stepped in with one foot between the two bamboo poles and the other outside. Just when the two men banged their poles together and could have smashed her foot in the process, she lifted it up and moved it away for a second or two. She moved her feet with such agility between the two pairs of heavy bamboo poles without ever looking down to where her feet were dancing to the rhythm created by the clicking sound of the bamboo poles as they hit the floor or slammed against each other. Then the rhythm began to quicken, and she moved faster in between the clicking poles.

Arthur dreaded looking. Surely she was going to be badly hurt; all it took for that to happen was a split-second delay in lifting her tiny feet. He was so relieved when the dance was over, which received loud cheers and applause. A band then took the stage.

A few minutes later, he noticed her with her shoes on that time weaving her way through the tables acknowledging with a radiant smile and bows the complimentary words people gave to congratulate her on her performance. To Arthur's surprise, she was heading toward their table. All the men stood up clapping. "Excellent, Didi!" "Fantastic, Didi." "Well done, Didi!"

Miguel grabbed a chair for her beside him and told Arthur, "Meet my sister Dolores." She nodded at him. "What would you like to drink, Didi?" Miguel asked.

"A soft drink, a Coke or a Pepsi. I don't want anything to eat now. I'm not hungry."

Arthur jumped up and insisted that he would fetch the drink. He came back with a tray of drinks for everybody, and she thanked him.

"Forgive me, but how should I call you, Dolores or Didi?" Arthur asked.

"It's the same thing. My name is Dolores Diaz. Some people took the abbreviation of both names and put them together, and DD became Didi, but you can call me anything you like."

Arthur was looking at her intently. In her national costume, she was even more beautiful and attractive than he had remembered. She mesmerized him; he wished he could whisk her away from this maddening crowd. If only he could be alone with her, get to know everything there was to know about her, he was sure he would readily fall in love with her, and if she reciprocated, their relation he was sure would not have the same unfulfilled ending he had had with Sonya.

His thoughts were interrupted by a band playing salsa tunes. Several people were dancing, but some withdrew when it shifted to rock music. A girl grabbed the microphone and in a lovely voice accompanied by the band began to sing "Memories." There was a rush to the dance floor. Arthur wasted no time. He asked Didi to dance. The dance floor was crammed. They hardly had space to move. He thought that might work in his favor. He could squeeze her to him. But that was not to be. She had bent her left arm so that her elbow would keep a distance between them.

He had her in his arms, but he was at a loss for words. He commented on the nice party, congratulated her on her dance, and mentioned that he had seen her at church the previous Sunday. She nodded in each case but said nothing. The song ended, and a man replaced the singing girl. In a harsh and out-of-tune tone, he sang what vaguely resembled "Only You." Arthur continued to dance. He told her that her brother had invited him after the church service the following day to see a family apartment that was up for rent.

"Apparently, it had been built for some member in the family who was getting married."

"That was me."

His heart sank.

"I was engaged, but we broke our engagement. I don't care what happens to that apartment. Can we sit?"

It was well past one in the morning when Arthur returned to his hotel room. He spent hours thinking of Didi. She must have been around twenty, he figured. Her looks, inviting as they were, were coupled with reserved behavior. It tortured him to think that when they danced, her lips he dreamed of embracing were so close to his, and her black hair he longed to stroke was touching his cheek. Her aristocratic neck he wished he could caress with his lips was only a shade away. Then there was her warm body he held so close that seemed so far away. What would he tell her if he saw her again?

The clock struck three. It was time he got some sleep. If only she would fade away. Maybe he should instead turn his thoughts to Lesley and his daughters. He tried hard to do so but found himself torn between the realities of his life and his imagined, newfound love. He tried to reason with himself. This must be a case of simple physical attraction compounded by his loneliness. *Why can't I just enjoy my feelings for Didi? Why am I being haunted by guilt and unnecessary remorse? I've done nothing wrong.* He looked at his watch. In a few hours, he would see the apartment. Then he would write Lesley a letter about it and tell her that he loved and missed her. *Yes, returning home to Lesley and the girls. That's what I should be thinking about.* Having sorted that out in his mind, he finally fell asleep.

When Arthur saw the apartment, he was enchanted and wasted no time in renting it. It was on the second floor and nicely furnished with new kitchen appliances. It had three bedrooms, a living room, and two bathrooms—a rather large place for a single person, but he could well afford it. Within a day, he moved in and converted one bedroom into a study. He liked his new environment and found Miguel and his family to be warm and friendly.

Soon, they invited him for dinner, where he met Miguel's mother. They talked about life on Mindanao, its shortcomings and many advantages. The economic situation was not good; there was high unemployment, and the Islamic insurgency was in the south. Yet life where they lived was unhurried and pleasant. Perhaps they did not make much money, but they were content with what they had, and that was their definition of happiness.

They mentioned how they enjoyed the camaraderie in the church community and how everybody could be relied on to provide help if someone was in need. They underlined what Mindanao had to offer—modern cities such as Davao and beautiful resorts like those on Samal and Talikud Islands. There were also the hot springs of Surigao del Sur and good fishing off the coast. Miguel and Ramon had been to Manila for a short visit and had taken Didi with them.

Didi listened throughout the conversation contributing only a few comments here and there. Arthur had tried to engage her in conversation on a few occasions, but she never gave him much of a chance. On her side, Didi had nothing against Arthur. If anything, she felt sorry for this lonely man so far from his family, but this traveled, better-educated foreigner inhibited her.

Arthur was starting his first car mechanics course in a nearby village, and Miguel had signed up for it. Arthur noticed how bright, shrewd, and popular he was among his classmates, who nicknamed him Mr. No Problem for he had the habit of preceding his answer to any query with "No problem."

When Arthur returned to his apartment, his thoughts invariably turned to Didi. He was obsessed with her. He wished he could see her everyday if for nothing else but to recharge his memory with her image, but she continued to be aloof. He wanted to penetrate that invisible barrier that seemed to surround her, *But how?* he wondered.

He was utterly taken aback when one afternoon there

was a knock at the door and there she was. "I brought your laundry," she said. They had agreed that her family would take care of his laundry.

"Please come in."

"I won't stay long."

She asked if he was enjoying the apartment and the city. The discussion then moved to the inevitable comparison with life in England and Wales. She listened attentively as he described it interrupting him with a question here and there.

"I long to travel. I envy you. I've never been out of this country. Do you know that there are over two million Filipina girls—I don't pretend to know the exact number—who are working abroad? They do all sorts of things. Many are university graduates, and yet they accept menial housework to support their families and to get the experience of traveling and living abroad. I wanted to apply myself just for the latter reason. I would never want to take on housework.

"There are other girls, you know, performing white-collar work as sales girls, in hotels, banks, and so on. That would appeal to me. My brothers are very protective of me. They have constantly objected to my being employed overseas pointing to news reports about certain countries in the Gulf region where the girls' passports are withheld as soon as they arrive and handed to them only after their contracts end. Even if they're mistreated or overworked, and the newspapers point out that some are, they cannot leave their employers or the country for that matter.

"Other cases were also reported where girls, who responded to advertisement for work in nearby Asian countries, found themselves on arrival in the clutches of prostitution rings from which escape was next to impossible.

So there you are. I dream of traveling and seeing other countries, but working abroad can sometimes be risky." She rose to leave. "I'm sorry. I stayed longer than I intended to."

"Oh, please no! I enjoyed our talk. I'd love to see you again to continue our discussion perhaps before the next laundry delivery."

"Maybe," she said with a giggle.

The following Sunday evening, she knocked at his door. He invited her in, but she declined. "Ramon and Miguel are with their girlfriends," she told him. "It's a nice evening. I was going for a walk and thought you might want to join me."

"But of course."

The sun had just dipped behind the horizon leaving its last orange rays on a cloud. Various insects joined in a humming sound interspersed by the chirps of hundreds of birds that drowned the noise of the fading traffic.

Didi wore tight blue jeans and a pale-blue blouse. The fitted jeans underscored the contours of her body. Arthur smelled the faint odor of the perfumed soap she used in the shower. Her makeup was not overly done. Her big, almond, black eyes scarcely needed to be enhanced by makeup. Her hair was neatly combed, and her lips wore a shade of subdued red.

The two walked along a road that led from their house to the outskirts of town.

"Tell me about yourself, Didi. I know very little about you."

"Well, as you may have gathered, I'm the only girl in the family and the youngest. I often feel spoiled. I was an average student or maybe slightly above average. Now that I finished high school, I feel a bit lost. I'd like to work, but opportunities in this small town are hard to come by. I probably could get a job in one of the resorts or one of the bigger cities on the island, but my brothers won't hear of it. They see me destined to get married and raise children."

"You were engaged, weren't you?"

"Yes." She sighed. "I still don't know what happened. Alfredo and I were in love, in fact very much in love. We were going to get married as soon as our apartment was ready, but then ... Well, a couple of months before, he broke our engagement saying he was not ready for the responsibility of settling down and raising a family."

"Maybe it was for the better."

"Why do you say that? Everybody liked Alfredo except perhaps my mother. He was fun with a warm disposition, and he was good looking too. My mother had reservations about him because he never held a job for very long. After that happened, I felt betrayed. At times, I wished I'd never met him. But we talked enough about me. Tell me about your wife, Arthur. You must miss her very much now that you haven't seen her for over a year."

He wished she had not dragged Lesley into the conversation. He wanted to talk about them and them alone. "As a matter of fact, I got married very young," he said defensively.

"So what does that have to do with it?"

"It's hard to explain, but maybe you did the right thing not getting married so young."

"But Arthur, I'm nineteen. You think I'm too young to be capable of sharing a mature love with a man?"

"I'm sure you're capable, but the person you love when you're nineteen or twenty is not the same person you want to love when you're older and more mature."

"Does this mean you don't love your wife anymore?"

"No, it's just that sometimes I feel my life has ended before it even started, my emotional life that is. I feel I'm now capable of so much love and emotion than when I got married at age twenty. I wasn't a man of the world then and probably not much better now. I remember proposing to my wife before even telling her I loved her."

"Did you love her then?"

"I probably did, but not with the passion and force in me at present."

"What happened after your marriage? Didn't your love develop and grow?"

"We cared for each other, and we still do very much, but here again, expressions and declarations of love became more muted. There were other priorities—work, pregnancies, children, and simply the realities of daily life. It's when I came to this country that I realized how affection and love need not be dampened by daily preoccupations. My emotions, which I had been brought up to conceal, now want to burst out. Didi, all I'm saying is that you have everything going for you. You have charm, beauty, youth, and poise. Any man would dearly love to have you. Take your time to choose."

"Any man? Does this include you? Are you flirting with me, Arthur?" she asked with a mischievous smile. She had noted his references to her beauty and his emotions. The baiting instinct was awakened in her. She enjoyed it. *Why not? It would be nice to play that game with a foreigner.*

Arthur gave her a broad smile and surprised himself with his answer. "I'm trying very hard to do so. I'm only human."

They had walked for half an hour or more and headed home. Miguel was there when she entered the house.

"Where were you, Didi?"

"I was walking with your professor."

"I think he has his eyes on you. I think he's fallen for you," he said with a big teasing grin. "Did he promise you eternal love?"

"Not quite," she said with a smile, "but you're right. I think he's fallen for me, so let him suffer," she said with a shrug and a giggle.

Arthur was happy that the ice between him and Didi had been broken. He wondered if she was able to detect how he felt about her. What bothered him though was her constant reference to Lesley. He had never had this same passionate feeling toward his wife he thought. Didi stirred deeply buried emotions in him and opened his sexual appetite. He wanted her, every bit of her.

He recalled his sexual experiences with Lesley. Her second pregnancy had become advanced during an unusually hot summer. They found it uncomfortable to share a narrow double bed. A neighbor was selling twin beds, and they bought them. They slept better, but the intimacy was gone. They were too inhibited to invite each other to share a bed. Besides, their favorite television programs came on late, and by the time they were over, they were sleepy, and sex was not usually in the cards. Their sexual encounters trickled to once every five or six weeks or less, and sometimes when they did it, it was as if each felt guilty toward the other for allowing so much time to lapse without it. Sex became a marital duty rather than real enjoyment.

Yet he could not help feeling guilty. He picked up a piece of paper and started a letter to Lesley.

My dear Les

I hope you are all keeping well. I am getting along fine here. My course is progressing well, and I am very happy in this apartment. The owners invited me to a lovely dinner at their place, and we had a long discussion about life in Mindanao. It was very enjoyable.

The weather continues to be hot and humid, but the rainy season is not here yet. It is hard to believe that a year has passed since we parted, but as you yourself said, time passes very quickly, and before you know it, the second year will be over as well.

All my love to you, Janet, and Mary. I miss you all.

Arthur

He read what he wrote. He did not like it. It sounded very perfunctory. He thought of tearing it up, but he realized he had not written for a while and decided to mail it just the same.

He sat in a more comfortable chair to sip a beer and fathom his feelings for Didi. It was not only physical attraction, he thought; he enjoyed immensely being with her. Would it not be wonderful if he could be with her every day, every single day of his life? He was definitely in love with her. *Oh God! Is there a cure for love?* But why was he appealing to God? Wasn't it in the house of God that he had first seen her? Maybe God wanted it that way. *No, it can't be. I'll go to church next Sunday, take communion, and pray for strength to overcome this overwhelming passion for her.*

When Didi retired to her room, she could not help thinking of Arthur. She was flattered that he was attracted to her. What should she do now? She has definitely matured since her teens and particularly since her broken engagement. When she met Alfredo, she was eighteen, but before that, she had baited a few classmates experimenting with sex with a couple of them. Alfredo was her first case of really mature love, and with marriage around the corner, there was not much inhibition in their encounters. When he broke the engagement, that experience shook her badly. From then on, she vowed, she would be on her guard with men.

But she enjoyed Arthur's company. He was different, mature, thoughtful, gentle, and not bad looking either. Why not see more of him? Nothing of consequence could happen anyway. He was already married and a father. A foreigner passing by, ten years her senior. It was a cul-de-sac relationship. Why does she not take it at that and continue to see him for companionship? Nothing more.

Over the following three weeks, Arthur and Didi met frequently. They talked about many things—the pace of life in their countries, religion, art, music, and their aspirations. Once in a while, as if seeking reassurance, she would tease him about his feelings for her, and when he would open up, she would gently remind him that he was married.

When Arthur returned to his room, he often put on paper his thoughts about Didi sometimes in a line or two or in one or more paragraphs, things he was too inhibited to tell her to her face. If she rebuffed him, he would lose face and she might put an end to their relationship altogether. Writing things down seemed to release his pent-up emotions.

Didi felt happier whenever she saw Arthur. He filled a void in her life. She was sure he was attracted to her and perhaps in love too, but she was less sure of how to handle that relationship. She could not get herself to put him off. Why not admit it? She missed him if she did not see him for a day or two. It was by no means like the passionate feelings she once held for Alfredo, *But could it be just a matter of time?* she wondered.

Then one evening when they stepped out of the house and walked silently for a few minutes, she suddenly took his hand in hers, stopped, looked at him, and said softly, "Tell me, Arthur. Are you in love with me?"

He could not take it anymore. He pulled her back to the house and up to his apartment. "I have something to show you." He opened a drawer, picked up a bunch of papers, and handed them to her. "Here. I wrote you many notes that I never had the courage to send."

"Notes? To me?" She picked up the first one and glanced quickly at the lines.

My dearest dear,

You asked me today if I was a jealous person. I lied when I said no. Yesterday, I saw you in the garden smelling a rose and felt jealous because it was close to your lips. I looked at your hair and felt jealous because it was caressing your neck. Above all, I felt jealous of your shadow because it was inseparable from your body.

She picked up another.

We walked today side by side, and talked about life. I said to myself, *Forgive me, God, but what would be the purpose of life if my Didi did not exist? Would life have been worth living without her?*

Before she could read others, he covered the rest of the notes with his hand. "Please don't read anything in front of me. It embarrasses me." He sighed and looked down. "Now you know."

She moved toward him, gave him a passing kiss on his lips, took her notes, and went down to her room. She went through them twice savoring every word. This was no longer a companionship. It had become serious. When she stepped into the living room, Miguel took one look at her and sensed something was wrong.

"What's the matter, Didi? Why do you look so pensive?"

She always confided in Miguel. "Nothing, really. It's just that Arthur told me he was in love with me."

"So what's new? I could have told you that myself. Does he propose to marry you?"

"How can he? He's already married, and you know that," she exclaimed impatiently.

"No problem. It happens all the time. There should be a way out. But first, are you in love with him? Do you want to marry him?"

"Those are two different questions. Ever since Alfredo, I've stopped giving my emotions free reign. I love with my brains now as much as with my heart. My brains tell me that he's a very nice person. He worships the ground I walk on and will spare no effort to make me happy. He's not bad looking. In fact, he's good looking in his own way. He's serious and steady, not like some of the characters around here, and he can take me away. Maybe we can live in Manila, or England. Yes, my brains tell me I could marry him. As for love, I don't know. I enjoy being with him and miss him if I don't see him for a couple of days. If that's love, it's nothing compared to how he feels about me."

"So you'd marry him then, but do you think he would propose to you if he were single?"

"How can I entice him to divorce his wife? You know our church ruling on divorce."

"Just ask him that question. Let me know, and give me time to think things over."

Didi showed up at Arthur's apartment the following day. "We've got to talk." He nodded and looked at her anxiously awaiting a verdict. "I read your notes. They're the most wonderful thing that has happened to me. Nobody has ever written me a love letter before. I will always treasure them. Arthur dear, you confided in me, so now it's my turn to confide in you. When I was engaged to Alfredo and so close to getting married, I dropped my guard at his insistence. I'm not the pure virgin girl you think I am."

She stopped to see the effect of her words. He did not react. "I have since learned my lesson. I don't want to fool you, Arthur, or lead you down a blind alley. I'm not prepared to have affairs with anybody. I want to save myself and my body for my future husband."

"How I envy him."

"Would you have wanted to marry me if you were single?"

"I would break hell and high water to marry you, Didi, if I were free."

"I've confided in Miguel about our predicament. He said he wanted time to think of something. I have no idea what he has in mind. In the meantime, let's not be gloomy.

Let's pretend we'll get married one day and dream about it." Noting his pensive mood, she added, "Arthur, I need a hug."

He hugged her and kissed her passionately, but then she slipped out of his arms and left.

Arthur knew full well how the Catholic Church— whether in Wales or the Philippines— stood on divorce. Divorce was next to impossible. He was aware that both civil marriage and divorce proceedings existed, but to him, the church rulings took precedence over man-made laws. Even if he followed the civil divorce path arduous as it might be, how could he explain this to Lesley and above all to his daughters, who doted on him? It was a hopeless case.

For the next two months, Didi and Arthur tried to imagine what their life together would be like—where they would live, what sort of work he would do, where they would travel. She told him she didn't want children for the first five years; she wanted to devote herself and keep herself totally for him.

Then the day came when Miguel said he had thought of a way and wanted to talk to them. When he explained his plan, Didi gasped but Arthur nodded agreement.

"Arthur, you must seriously think about what I'm proposing. Take a week to do so."

Two days later, Arthur told Miguel that he was ready to play his part. All that mattered was to be able to spend the rest of his life with Didi. He had long since lost the will to think rationally.

The Road of No Return

Shrewd, calculating Miguel kept loose contact with a militant group fighting for the establishment of an Islamic state in the southern Philippines. Though the Abu Sayyaf group belonged to a religion and ideology different from his, they had on occasion launched terrorist activities not far from their town. He wanted to keep his options open and was proven right.

In a surprise move, several years earlier, the Abu Sayyaf group raided Kipagah; they emptied a couple of banks coffers, blew up a telephone exchange, and took some people hostage to cover their withdrawal. Miguel's business, home, and family were spared. What he did was to offer on more than one occasion free car repairs to two of the group's sympathizers and to join them in chorus when they expressed disgust with government corruption. Now he wanted to be paid back. He had a scheme that could not be implemented without their cooperation. There were also financial arrangements to be discussed.

"To play their part, they wanted two hundred thousand pesos," he told Arthur. "I managed to bring it down to a hundred and fifty thousand all inclusive. Can you manage that, Arthur? If so, you should start withdrawing money from the bank soon and gradually empty the account."

In fact, Miguel had negotiated a lower deal agreeing with them on 130,000 pesos. He wanted to keep 20,000 pesos for his pains.

Over the previous fourteen months, Arthur had saved from his salary in dollars and pesos what amounted to about 200,000 pesos. He had kept that discreet as he wanted to surprise Lesley and the girls by inviting them to visit the Philippines and nearby places in Asia. Apart from these savings were 50,000 pesos in the petty cash, which nobody knew about except himself. He could borrow them now and return them later. In all, he had 250,000 pesos. If he paid 150,000 out, he would be left with a 100,000 pesos to start a new life. He readily paid Miguel the requested advance for the operation with the understanding that the rest would be paid at a later date directly to the Abu Sayyaf people when everything was ready.

Two months passed before a man showed up at Miguel's garage to tell him that the merchandise would be delivered two days later. He gave a description as to where and when. Everything then went into high gear. Arthur, Didi, and Ramon, the only three who apart from Miguel knew the details of the scheme, were informed immediately.

That evening, Miguel invited a few friends over with Arthur for drinks at his house. Halfway through the evening, Arthur, playing his part, mentioned that he wanted to head out the following afternoon to a village about fifty kilometers away to invite participation in one of his forthcoming courses. He could go only in the late afternoon as he was working before then. He understood that it was a beautiful mountainous area and that there was a nice guesthouse nearby. He would spend the night there and head to the village early the following morning.

He wasn't sure of the exact road to follow as there were several rural dirt roads zigzagging in and out the few villages in the area. A couple of persons volunteered to explain while others admitted that they had not been there since the troubles had begun.

It was at this juncture that Ramon said he would lead Arthur to the guesthouse and return leaving him there. Arthur said how much he was enjoying his stay in Mindanao and that he was planning to bring his family from Wales to visit in the next few months. The discussion then drifted to other subjects among them the insurgency movement, but as there had been a lull in the fighting for months, that subject was quickly dropped.

The following morning, Arthur showed up for his class. He tried to behave as normally as possible. In the afternoon, he started packing. He filled a small sports bag with what a person would normally need for an overnight stay. In a second duffel bag, he packed many of his belongings. He left behind relics of his past in England—his tweed jacket and wool pants, his English boots, his formal shirts, a couple of sports shirts and some underwear, family pictures, Lesley's letters, and his work papers. He filled a third small plastic bag with items he was instructed to bring.

By then it was 6:30 p.m. There was a knock at the door. It was Didi. She looked nervous, anxious, and worried. "Arthur darling, is there anything I can do? Can I help in any way?"

He shook his head and looked at his watch. "Two hours from now, I'll be dead." He sounded very serene. "But there will be life after death you know. We'll meet in the next life and live together happily ever after." He said it casually trying hard to show no emotions.

She hugged him tightly. "Arthur darling, you're the most wonderful man in the world. I know now for sure and more than ever that I'm madly in love with you. Take care of yourself. May God bless and guide you."

They hugged for a couple of minutes only to be interrupted by another knock at the door. It was Ramon inquiring if Arthur was ready.

Arthur put his two bags in the Toyota. The plastic bag he carried contained his wedding ring, watch, sunglasses, and the cross and chain he always wore under his shirt. It was the same cross he had received for his first communion. As instructed, he also brought a can of grease and put an empty jerry can in the car.

By then it was dusk. They waited a bit more while the last lights of the day gradually faded. Ramon looked at his watch and signaled it was time to go. Didi gave Arthur another big hug. He felt her salty tears on his cheek.

Then it was Miguel's turn. "Arthur, it takes a courageous man, someone very much in love to do what you're doing for there can be no return once you start down this road. God be with you."

They hugged and patted each other's back. Arthur started the engine and followed Ramon. They made a point of stopping at a nearby gas station, where Arthur filled up his car with gas as well as the jerry can. He told the man at the station where he was going adding that he always liked to carry extra gasoline because of his frequent travels in rural areas, where gas stations were not always available. They then set out.

Ramon took the lead. About fifty minutes later, they were in hilly terrain. Ramon noticed a car parked on the side of the road with its back lights blinking and its hood up. He slowed down and put his blinkers on twice as a signal to Arthur, who parked right behind it. Ramon passed the stalled car and noticed two men huddled under the hood as if examining the engine. There was a sharp turn in the road at that point. Ramon stopped his car a good fifty yards down the road, switched off his lights, and waited. Traffic had been light when they had left town, and out where they were, it was almost nonexistent due to the fear of terrorist activity.

Things happened very quickly. Arthur stepped down taking the duffel bag with him and leaving the sports bag in his car. The two men asked him if he had brought what they wanted. He gave them the plastic bag and pointed out the grease and the jerry can. They took the items in the bag, opened the trunk, and huddled in it for a minute. Arthur and Ramon were keeping an eye on the road.

The two men soon emerged with a body, which they put in the driver's seat of the Toyota. He was wearing Arthur's cross, watch, and wedding ring. They quickly smeared him but particularly his head and his hands with grease adding some grease as well to the car's floor. They doused him with gasoline from the jerry can and spread it thoroughly inside the car. They left the gasoline can open and almost a quarter full in the Toyota. Then they signaled to Arthur to get quickly in their trunk. They then pushed Arthur's Toyota down the hill at the sharp turn in the road. They watched briefly as the car burst into flames and then drove on with Arthur in the trunk. The whole operation took less than three minutes.

It was now Ramon's turn to act. After looking at the flames

for a good ten minutes, he drove slowly to the nearest village with a police station. He went in showing great anxiety. Two policemen were on duty.

"I was leading my neighbor! He's an Englishman who wanted to go to the guesthouse. There was a bend in the road." He told them where it was. "When I looked in my rearview mirror after the bend, I didn't see him. I retraced my way several meters back and saw his white Toyota in flames down the hill. I've come for help. I have no idea if he's dead or alive."

A good twenty minutes passed before a policeman could ready himself to go with Ramon. By the time they reached the smoldering car, almost three-quarters of an hour had passed since it had gone up in flames. They went down the hill with a flashlight. "He's dead all right," the policeman said, "burned totally I would say beyond recognition. You'd better come back to the station with me to give me his name and address as well as yours. We'll send an investigator tomorrow morning to write the usual report. He may contact you for it."

With his flashlight going over the charred corpse, he saw something shining and picked it up. "It's his cross. I recognize it. He always wore it," said Ramon.

"Let's collect any other items of value before passers-by clean them up."

The policeman picked up a mangled wristwatch and with great difficulty managed to release a partially melted wedding ring from the dead man's finger.

An hour later, Ramon arrived home to announce to Miguel and Didi that everything had gone OK. "Arthur's dead, burned beyond recognition."

"This calls for a celebration," exclaimed Miguel.

Didi was less euphoric. After all, his fate lay in the hands of the Abu Sayyaf group, and anything could go wrong.

When the trunk closed on him, Arthur panicked. At first, he felt claustrophobic; maybe there was not enough oxygen. Sweat gathered on his forehead. His cramped body ached from the position he had to take to fit in such a confined space. Then it hit him. The trunk had just held a dead man. He smelled the stench of death, or was it his imagination? He was scared. He knew nothing about these two Abu Sayyaf men driving him. *Can they be trusted? What if they don't live up to their end of the bargain? It would be easy for them to rob me and do me in.* No questions would be asked since he was already presumed dead in his own burning car. His heart raced faster. He thought he could hear his heartbeat. He was sweating profusely. He did his best to lessen the effect of the beating his body was taking on the bumpy ride. He figured that the car was by then taking dirt roads and avoiding the relatively smoother main road.

Close to an hour later, the car came to a halt and he was let out of the trunk. Taking a deep whiff of fresh air, he looked around and saw the shadows of two other armed men in front of two thatched-roof cottages. His drivers motioned him to enter one of the cottages. There, two more men sat inside. It was a scantly furnished room. A wire hanging from the ceiling held a dim light bulb. A table doubled for a desk and a dining place. The cigarette smoke was overpowering; tens of butts lay in a small clay dish. A Kalashnikov was leaning casually against the wall. A few boxes and a camp bed filled the remaining space. A lean person with hollow eyes who appeared to be of a higher rank as he did all the talking motioned him to sit on one of the two chairs left. He examined Arthur with a piercing look and with the faint hint of a smile broke the silence. "Welcome. My name is Abu Ali. Did you bring the money?"

Arthur nodded. Miguel had told him that the agreement called for him to pay 80,000 pesos after his presumed death was carried out successfully as a second installment. Miguel had already delivered the agreed-to first installment. Arthur handed over the money. He was kept in the dark as to the following steps. All he knew was that he would be united with Didi sometime in the near future. He was anxious to ask about that, but he waited until Abu Ali finished counting the money.

"Good. Did you bring the picture?" Abu Ali asked.

Arthur handed him a passport-size photograph.

"In two or three days, you will get your identity card. You will take the identity of the dead man. We will take care of replacing the picture and making the necessary touches. Destiny has strange ways of arranging things. Your new name is almost like your old. The dead man was called Arturo." He smiled. "Arturo Fernandez."

"How did he die?"

"He deserved to die. He was an informer. We kill informers. Once in a while, we get cases like this. Only in your case, this was a special order. We had to wait for someone whose height matched more or less yours, and we did not kill him by a bullet. He was stabbed. It is messier than a bullet, but we did not want to leave holes in his skull or bones. We delivered the goods as promised."

"What will happen next?"

"You will be our guest for a few weeks."

"A few weeks?" Arthur exclaimed.

"Not in this place. You will stay here for a few days, and then we will take you to a more secure island. After that, we shall see. Maybe three or four weeks later, we will deliver you to Miguel at Cebu, and that will be the end of our association."

"But I don't really have the features of a Filipino with a name like Arturo Fernandez."

"This country is a melting pot of races—Muslim, Malay, Chinese, Spanish. Nobody will ask you, and anyway, you do not owe an explanation to anybody. If you have to give one, you can say that your mother was British, that you went to school in England and lived there for a while. Simple, isn't it? Now just relax and try to enjoy your stay. We cannot promise you first-class accommodations. We are fighting a war, not running a hotel."

Four days later, Abu Ali showed up to see Arthur. He was in a talkative mood. He told him that his funeral had been held and that he would be leaving that night to a more secure southern island. He would not name it. "One day, we will have our country, and then we will not have to hide or do things in a clandestine manner," Abu Ali said as he lit a cigarette.

"Do you have a reasonable chance of doing so?"

"God is on our side because God is just. Mindanao and several southern islands have been home for our Muslim population for centuries. We lived in harmony with nature, but then the Spaniards came, and then the Americans followed by the Japanese during the last war, and then the Americans came back. The indigenous population watched one occupier replace another for years. When independence came, they hoped that would bring prosperity and tranquility to their lives, but that was not to be.

"Streams of migrants from other parts of the country, mostly Christians, flowed into Mindanao turning us Muslims into a minority in our own homeland. And that is not all. We are being governed whether from Manila or by the Manila lackeys here by an inept and a corrupt regime where one dictator or governor replaces another each one keen on enriching himself and his entourage and all of them with no interest at all in the needs of the people. We feel that the only way out is to turn back to the fundamental system of values embodied in Islam. This way, we can build a society based on mutual assistance rather than greed. A Muslim has to set aside a certain percentage of his income, a *zakat*, to help the needy and the poor. We try to enforce this though some people look at it as a form of taxation, but it is their obligation toward others."

"But is part of this money also used to buy arms and ammunition?" Arthur asked politely.

"This war has been forced on us. Nobody will hand us our rights." Abu Ali responded while drawing a deep smoke from his cigarette. "We have to fight for what we believe in. Muslim brothers from other countries contribute to our cause, and we raise some by our own means. Don't think that we use any means to raise money. We are not in the drug or illicit traffic business.

"We investigated you before deciding to help you. Although you are a Christian, you have been working to improve the lot of the poor from both religions. We figure, therefore, that the deal we made with you and Miguel was fair and of mutual interest since we too concentrate our efforts on the poor, who are the most neglected and the most alienated by government actions. The money we got from you will go to the poor and help subsidize our fighters, who are waging this relentless battle against injustice. Even if it takes a hundred years, we will prevail.

"Our strength is built on our beliefs. We are strong believers in God and his prophet. Infidels and nonbelievers try to subject everything in life to the test of logic and proof. For us, a belief takes precedence over trying to prove one thing or another is right or wrong. That can come later. Have we not harnessed light and fire without thoroughly understanding their nature? Have we not harvested and consumed our crops before exploring in depth the nature of plants and their usefulness? I urge you to follow the path of rightness and believe without questioning in God and his prophet, for that will lead to your salvation.

"I often hear people say that we believe in God and pray regularly, but that has not led to a just society. To them, I say a society is nothing but the summation of individuals and their leaders. If each one of them believed in justice, knew how to differentiate between right and wrong, and followed the right path indicated by our religion, society as a whole would become more just. It is not only how many times one prays that counts; it is one's beliefs and actions that will promote a better society."

Arthur did not readily respond. His curiosity was aroused however. "What about the Abu Sayyaf movement? How did it start?"

"Abu Sayyaf, God bless his soul, was a holy man. He left this country first to go to Libya to further his knowledge of Arabic and Islam. A couple of years later, he went to Saudi

Arabia. He spent several years there deepening his study of Islam with religious scholars. He marveled at a society governed by Islamic law and admired how Islam in the seventh century spread through North Africa and southern parts of Europe through the Arab conquest of these lands, conquest accomplished by the sword. He came back determined to defend his people and their religion in this country. He took the name Abu Sayyaf, which literally translated from Arabic means father of the sword. Several years after establishing his movement, he welcomed martyrdom when God willed it, but his movement keeps going with the same fervor it had when he established it."

Abu Ali took a final drag on his cigarette and threw the butt away leaving Arthur to his thoughts.

Arthur was a simple man. He was incapable of holding a debate over religious beliefs and social justice. Still, over the following weeks and on several occasions, he turned over in his mind Abu Ali's words. It all sounded simple and convincing—having a separate country where people would abide by religious dicta and moral values and extend mutual assistance to each other, but was this attainable in our modern society, or was it utopia pure and simple? He was inhibited from raising several questions that came to mind at the time as he felt it was not prudent to do so. It was not the high standards of morality that various religions advocated that bothered him, far from it. It was the interpretation given to the holy books whether in Islam, Christianity, or other religions issued as edicts by some purists that frightened him. In fact, he thought that in their zeal, such people might pose a threat to the very religion they were trying to protect.

Would any conceived and aspired-to society based on

dogma tolerate freedom of expression? And in achieving their goals, did the ends justify the means in the case of Abu Sayyaf? He thought of the poor informer who was killed to protect a movement based on a religious doctrine. Taking a human life was a prerogative of God, not other humans at will abiding by their own rules.

How about other acts? Forging his identity papers, robbing banks, kidnapping for ransom to raise money for the cause? Do movements based on ideology sometimes gradually drift to criminal acts as a means to promote their survival? And in doing so, doesn't the gap between ideology and demonstrated illicit action increasingly grow to the point of making this ideology less and less relevant?

He also thought of forcing or persuading other segments of the population to abide by certain codes of conduct based on dicta; he had women in mind. Had women's contributions to society been curtailed in some societies as a result? Had their rights in terms of dress code, access to education and employment, and taking their fate into their own hands on parity with men been sidestepped as a result?

Once more, he thought of the Abu Sayyaf group and whether there was another way to achieve their ends without recourse to violence that killed innocent bystanders. Were there other ways for them to achieve their objectives?

Democracy could provide an answer, but what if a country was in the grips of a ruthless dictator or one who paid just lip service to democracy? Would an armed struggle be justified? He had no answer to the questions. How could he describe the Abu Sayyaf group? Was it a militant action in the name of social justice or another form of dictatorship under the guise of religion? How did the members of the group feel after committing violent acts? How about that person who stabbed that informer? Was there such a thing as a singular feeling of guilt, or did that feeling dissipate if the actor felt it was shared by all the members of his group? These and other points kept him mentally alert during the following weeks when he was kept in relative isolation.

It was around eight at night that same day of Abu Ali's visit that two men showed up at his cottage and asked him to get into a car. Both bore handguns. It took them two hours to reach a deserted beach in southeast Mindanao. There in the dim light of a crescent moon occasionally masked by a passing cloud. Arthur, in the company of an armed guard, embarked on a small fishing boat that had another person aboard. The second armed guard drove away. They set sail on a relatively calm sea leaving the shores and hills of Mindanao, which were gradually engulfed in darkness. Arthur could not sleep. His fate was in the hands of two strangers leading him to an unknown destination. Moreover, the wind became a bit more active. As they gathered speed, the boat continued to override waves with splashes and drizzles of salt water frequently wetting his face.

At first light, they reached an island, and he was taken to a cottage with a cot, where he collapsed into a deep sleep.

Arthur's stay on that island, he thought, was the longest of his life. His guards had stern faces. They were not talkative, and they tried to keep him inside for a good part of the day. A monotonous diet of fish and rice kept him alive but dampened his spirits further. How he longed for a cold beer in this tropical heat, but alcohol was definitely forbidden in this strictly Muslim environment.

Flies and mosquitoes took turns harassing him day and

night. The cottage was a good two hundred meters from the water. He saw the azure water and observe the lush green vegetation all around. He asked for and was allowed to take a swim daily but only after sunset. The warm, penetrating sunlight woke him up as soon as the sun rose. No sooner had he washed than he was already sweating. He often tried to catch a breeze by sitting under a coconut tree, but wherever there was a shade, flies became more aggressive.

Three weeks later, Abu Ali showed up and informed him that the way was clear for his departure to Mindanao the following evening in the same manner in which he had arrived—by fishing boat. One of the men who engineered his death would meet him and drive him to the provincial town of Cagayan de Oro, a city Arthur had not visited before. They would arrive in time to take an internal flight to Cebu, where he would be handed over to Miguel.

Lesley was late coming home that evening. It was Friday, and she had stopped for her weekly groceries. At home, she was told there was a letter addressed to her on the mantel. She picked it up. It was from the Philippines, but Arthur's handwriting was not on the envelope. She read the letter and collapsed in her chair sobbing uncontrollably.

Dear Mrs. Jones,

It is with great sadness and a profound sense of regret that I have to convey to you the sad news of your husband's death as a result of a road accident on the evening of the 2nd of November 1981. In the short time that he had been with us, he had made a most significant contribution to improving the lot of many poor people in rural areas. He was respected, admired, and liked by everybody who knew him. May God rest his soul in peace.

I flew to Mindanao and conducted with Fr. Angel the funeral services and saw to his burial. It pains me to tell you that as a result of the accident, his car burst into flames and he was burned beyond recognition. I have made some discreet inquiries and was told the cost of shipping his body would be around £2,500. It is for this reason that I decided to have Arthur buried here among the people he loved and who loved him. If you wish the body to be exhumed and flown to England, please let me know.

Once more, please accept on behalf of all his trainees and myself our deepest sympathies and convey the same to your daughters.

Rev. A. Ramos.

After breaking the news to her daughters, Lesley took a few days to gather her thoughts. She read Ramos's letter a few times. A key phrase was his reference to the cost of shipping the body. To the cost he mentioned should be added the cost of a funeral and burial in Britain. This could bring the total cost of burial home to well over £4,500, a sum she could not afford especially now with a reduced income and two girls to raise. Lesley opted for a memorial service in town for Arthur instead.

Arthur kept reminding himself that he was at that point Arturo Fernandez, and on checking in at the hotel in Cebu, he first formally used this new identity and invented a new signature. Miguel and Didi were anxiously waiting for him in their hotel room.

"Arthur, my darling!" Didi screamed as she ran to hug him.

"Don't forget," he said, "Arthur's dead. I'm now Arturo Fernandez." He hugged her as tightly as he could feeling her wet cheeks and mixing his tears with hers.

For the previous three months, ever since his death had been planned, Arthur had been tense. He had lived through uncertainty in the company of militants for over a month. The sudden release of tension overpowered him. He wanted to cry out of happiness and a feeling that the ordeal was over. He kept reminding himself that he was a free man ready to start a new life with the person he passionately loved. What a wonderful feeling it was to love to the point of sacrificing everything, even your very existence, for a person who meant so much to you.

Miguel had found a priest who would marry them. All three went to see him that afternoon, and it was agreed that the wedding would take place three days later. Arturo, though anxious for the event to take place, was grateful for this breather. He could use it to rest physically and emotionally.

Miguel and Didi wanted to hear all the details he could give them about his adventure. In turn, Miguel described in detail Arthur's well-attended funeral including the eulogy given by Ramos.

Arturo felt sad in a way that he was abandoning his students and his mission he had enjoyed so much. He wondered how Lesley and his girls would take the news. *Did I do the right thing?* There was no use brooding about it. It was done and finished with. Didi's beautiful smile assured him that it was all worthwhile, and so on a partly cloudy morning on December 15, 1981, Dolores Diaz wed Arthur Jones alias Arturo Fernandez in Cebu.

Life after Death

Love is wonderful. After all, without it, how could we have come to life? Arthur thought as he pressed Didi against him feeling her body. Nobody in the world could have been happier than he was; of that he was certain.

"Didi, the love of my life, I don't think I ever lived before I met you."

"Do you really love me that much?"

"I love you more than I am ever capable of expressing. I can't believe that three days have passed since we married. Where has the time gone? If only I could stop the clock."

"You naughty boy! Haven't you had enough lovemaking? You could burn yourself out too quickly!"

"Don't tease me. Or on second thought, tease me more often. I love it."

"It's only the beginning. I'm really going to spoil you and make you forget everybody else but me."

"But I have," said Arturo guessing what she was alluding to. "Ever since I took that car ride with the Abu Sayyaf people, I never looked back. It's strange and tragic at the same time. You know, I've never once thought of Lesley. I spend most of the time focusing on the future, our future together. Are you happy, Didi?"

"I'm not saying. I want to keep you guessing. Do you realize that soon it will be Christmas and then New Year's and here we are in a city where we know nobody? We should plan a little celebration of our own."

"If I had enough money, we could have gone to Hong Kong and spent the holidays there. But I promise you it will be different next year when I become well off."

"And how do you propose to do that?" she asked with her finger straying on his lips.

"I did a considerable amount of thinking particularly during my stay on that island. You always wanted to go to Manila. We'll fly there after the holidays or before if you wish. I want to start my own business. I know how to fix things. I could work on my own, perhaps undertake repairs and maintenance for homeowners. There should be a need for such a service.

"Maybe I could sell my services by printing a flyer indicating that I am British trained and experienced and listing the range of services I offer. I'd circulate it only in the wealthier suburbs of Manila. I can handle electrical repairs, plumbing, and minor masonry. I could also hire somebody for air conditioning and maybe another for appliance repairs. I think I'll call my company Property Maintenance Services."

His enthusiasm was growing by the minute, but then he paused, and an expression of helplessness and gloom crossed his face.

"What's the matter? What's bothering you?"

"I guess I let my imagination lead me too far. All this will require capital. I need to buy some tools and equipment, rent a place, hire two or three people, buy a car, on and on. All I have now is less than a hundred thousand pesos. That has to cover our living expenses in Manila."

Didi, who had been carried away to fantasy land with him, refused to get back to earth so abruptly or at least not so quickly. "I'll help. I could answer the phone, take messages, and arrange appointments. We could start small. Maybe you could work on your own at first. If a job comes that you can't handle, then perhaps you could give it to somebody else to do on a commission basis."

Arturo shook his head. "That's not enough. We need money to start that sort of business."

"I remember Miguel mentioning on a couple of occasions that the government has ongoing programs to assist people who want to start their own businesses. This includes providing them with capital. At the time, he had deplored the fact that people in Manila had a better chance of getting such assistance than people in Mindanao or at least in our city. I have a feeling he mentioned something about the money being in the form of loans. Why don't we phone Miguel and get more information?"

It was two days before Miguel had made inquiries and returned their call. It turned out that there were several organizations providing assistance to small business owners and to the self-employed. These ranged from government-sponsored institutions to voluntary organizations. Miguel was not sure how the funds for a new venture were provided or on what terms, but he suggested that whatever organization they selected for assistance could guide them in that respect.

Arturo and Didi sought more information from the local government office in Cebu, reviewed their options, and decided to direct their inquiry to the Industries Institute of the University of the Philippines. With that behind them, they concluded that it served little purpose to keep worrying about the future. They would have plenty of time to do so once they got to Manila. Instead, they wanted to enjoy the holiday season in Cebu. They were poor but happy.

Through the church, they met a family they liked and were invited to share Christmas dinner with them. They went loaded with gifts. Several relatives and friends were also invited. Everybody was in a festive mood. The numerous children at the party had brought their Christmas toys and were playing with each other and mingling with the adults. Nobody seemed unnecessarily inquisitive about them. Their hostess had introduced them as friends who decided to spend the holiday season in Cebu on their way to Manila from Mindanao. People they had never met before greeted them warmly and engaged then in conversation about life in Mindanao. Drinks were served, and a sumptuous meal awaited them. Jokes, laughter, and music made for a jovial and a merry Christmas, one to cherish and remember.

Yet seeing all the children evoked many emotions in Arturo. He could not help thinking of his two girls. He missed them terribly. He recalled the many Christmases they had spent together as a family, the excitement Janet and Mary showed during the whole preceding week, the wishes they always made for a white Christmas, the gifts opening interspersed with hugs and kisses, the Christmas dinner often shared with one or two other couples.

Suddenly, he was full of remorse. He felt as if the umbilical cord that had tied him to his family in Wales had been severed for good, and he felt confused, depressed, and scared. He tried to reason with himself. He knew that he loved Didi madly, but he wondered if he had been blinded by his love to have paid such a high price for it. He probably would not be able to see Janet and Mary again. They would grow and mature without him. What had happened to his ethical upbringing? To his high standards? Morals? His commitment to church teachings and to his students he had so abruptly abandoned? Should he go back? But how? As Miguel had told him—as if he needed a reminder—he had embarked on a road from which there could be no return.

On the other hand, he loved being in the Philippines, the warmth of the people, the climate, the easygoing lifestyle. Didi was charming, terribly attractive, and sensual, and she wanted to contribute fully to their life together. That unknown and exciting life lying ahead of them was there for them to build together, to share and enjoy. Why should he be a prisoner of the past? He was a changed person. He was no longer the shy, self-effacing human being he had once been. He could no longer be satisfied with the rather dull life he had led back home.

As for his morals, he would retain them under his new name and continue to be the honest person he had always been. Was it really a crime to leave Lesley? He was not the first or the last person in the world to do so. If only religious dogma on divorce were more lenient in his church, he would not have had to fake his death.

He thought about his students. There should be no particular problem replacing him. As soon as he earned some money, he would send Ramos a contribution to the project that would more than cover the petty cash he had borrowed. He should stop torturing himself and work for a bright and enjoyable life ahead. That line of reasoning helped reassure him at least for the time being.

Arturo and Didi spent their time in Cebu exploring the city, window-shopping, discovering restaurants, and going to the movies. Not only was it Christmas; it was also their honeymoon, and they wanted to enjoy it to the fullest. They had no commitments or deadlines; they simply wanted to enjoy doing what they felt like doing at their own pace.

For New Year's, they decided to sacrifice part of their savings by booking a table for a dinner dance at one of the better Cebu hotels. They enjoyed the show, danced a lot, and drank to their everlasting happiness. They returned to their hotel clutching each other in the early hours of the morning.

But as everything else, it had to come to an end. It was time to leave Cebu and head for Manila. As the plane taxied for takeoff, Didi held Arturo's hand. Looking out the window, she murmured, "Cebu, city of love, goodbye."

"We shall return. I promise you that."

"I'll forever treasure our days here, for it was here that we married, had our honeymoon, and spent our first Christmas together. I love you, my Arturo."

"And I adore you, but the honeymoon isn't over yet." He pressed her hand gently.

Four months passed in Manila before they got settled. It was not easy for them to find their way among the 10 million others in the sprawling metropolis. They leased a modest, small apartment and furnished it sparingly with used or rented furniture. Arturo bought a secondhand scooter, which allowed him to take Didi around or use the backseat for his toolbox.

They visited the Industries Institute but were told that they could not be recommended for a loan before attending a training course for small-business entrepreneurs and preparing a business plan for their venture. Didi wanted to attend that course with Arturo, and he reluctantly agreed. She wanted to share the excitement of a working life, something she had never done before.

The next course started a month later. Sixteen other trainees had enrolled. They learned how to keep books, the problems of cash flow and money management, the procedures for registering and starting small businesses, how to determine the selling price of their products and services, and how to calculate their costs and estimate their profits.

Each person was then required to prepare a business plan for his or her venture and in doing so could seek advice from his or her trainer. Didi and Arturo felt a great sense of accomplishment when their plan was accepted and endorsed for a loan from the Development Bank of the Philippines.

Another six weeks passed before the bank approved their loan. Arturo spent his time running after the loan, selecting and buying tools, and preparing a flyer to advertise his business. Didi in the meantime was busy handling the bureaucracy involved in registering the business, securing permits, and obtaining a phone line. She proved good at it; in three months, all the hurdles were overcome. They had decided to work initially from their apartment.

Every evening, they exchanged news of their activities and their plans for the following day and shared their dreams for a bright future. It was all very exciting leaping into the unknown, and in their dreams, the bright hope of success more often than not overshadowed their fear of failure.

Everything was ready. Didi and Arturo spent three days going from house to house and apartment to apartment in a well-off suburb of Manila to distribute their flyers. These listed the services they offered and emphasized Arturo's British training and promised quick and efficient services at reasonable prices. There was nothing more to do except to wait for the phone to ring.

They spent three days glued to their chairs. Finally, the phone rang, and Didi jumped to answer it but soon hung up in frustration. It had been a wrong number. Had their work all been in vain?

A few hours later, their sagging morale got a jolt. It was a business call—their first. Arturo was on his scooter in a second. Two hours later, he returned beaming and holding two bottles of St. Miguel to celebrate his first earnings only to find an equally beaming Didi, for there had been two more calls. They were overjoyed that night as they began to count and recount their day's earnings. How wonderful life was. Anxiety was being replaced by confidence. Their success modest as it was or maybe because it was propelled their love for each other to new heights.

Business grew gradually but steadily. Word of mouth spread that Arturo was a reliable, courteous, and obliging handyman. Didi took the calls, arranged his schedule, and kept the books. He concentrated on the technical aspects of his work.

Eight months later, he sent Ramos a donation of 75,000 pesos from an anonymous donor as a contribution to Arthur's former project. That was one and a half times the amount he had taken from the petty cash. By year's end, they had made sufficient money to permit them to move to more comfortable accommodations, buy a van, rent premises for their business, and hire a helper.

He took her to Hong Kong for Christmas. He traveled on his British passport using his original name and had no problems. They went on a shopping spree and indulged themselves sampling many of the Chinese delicacies in Hong Kong and Kowloon restaurants. Arturo bought her a heavy golden chain for Christmas. She in turn bought him a silk tie and two beautiful shirts. They remembered their previous Christmas in Cebu and bought a suitable present to mail to their former hosts on their return to Manila. Life, though increasingly hectic, was enjoyable, and the trip to Hong Kong gave them a breather.

The second-year results exceeded their wildest dreams. Arturo had by then three helpers. He had preferred to recruit fresh graduates from technical schools shaping their knowledge to his expectations. His two fastest growing areas of business were air conditioning maintenance and the repair and servicing of appliances. His first helper was a specialist in air conditioning having had three years of experience. He was the only experienced person he had hired, but as that part of the business expanded, he hired a fresh graduate to work with him and learn from him.

Appliances were a different matter. They ranged from such things as blenders, mixers, and toasters to refrigerators, washing machines, and dishwashers. In several cases, Arturo had to tell his clients that some of their equipment was beyond repair or that because they were too old, spare parts were unavailable or the cost of repairs did not justify performing a repair.

For months, he had been turning over an idea. After

many inquiries and calculations and several discussions with Didi, he decided to put it into effect. He rented a large store in one of the better areas of Manila establishing a separate business in his name, which he called "Appliances. Discount Sales and Repair." He had been in touch with wholesalers of well-known and popular brands, and as a result, he was able to fill the store with an array of appliances on consignment. In that way, he could offer his clients new appliances for sale in lieu of costly repairs or lure them to buy new products by underscoring the advantages of the newer models. He also offered various discounts, "fidelity discounts" for established customers, "friendly" cash discounts, and special "super sales clearances."

Didi opted to work in the store. Always well dressed and groomed and attractive with an outgoing personality, she excelled at engaging customers and haggling over discounts before closing a deal. Arturo concentrated on maintenance and repairs offering as well maintenance contracts.

Four years later, he had two vans and six employees working in a repair shop nearby and serving homes in various districts of Manila. He also engaged a full-time bookkeeper and office worker. But the store was their biggest money maker. They moved into a comfortable home that they furnished tastefully, and they had two new cars. A cook and a maid were also hired. Their life seemed to be easy sailing. Didi took a few shopping trips to Hong Kong and Singapore by herself. Arturo could not join her because he was putting in ten to twelve hours a day and working many weekends.

With success came a new lifestyle. For Arturo, the hectic pace meant that he often returned home late at night tense and exhausted. He could not be counted on to show up for lunch or at regular hours in the evening. They often had their meals separately. He looked forward to the weekend to catch up on some sleep and rest, but often, that was not possible as he had to deal with emergency phone calls or had to decide and prepare orders for spare parts and new appliances.

Didi, while very busy during her working hours, had a more regular schedule tied to the store's opening and closing hours. More often than not, she returned to an empty home. When he came home, they exchanged news of the day but somehow did not have much else to say to each other.

On Sundays, she went mostly alone to church. They joined a sports club ostensibly to enjoy their weekends, but after two or three outings, she found herself going to the swimming pool alone. They had many acquaintances but hardly any true friends. They had no time to nurture a deep friendship. Once in a while, they entertained at their home and were entertained in return. These were enjoyable occasions but not frequent enough.

Didi began to slowly realize that something had changed in their life. She had everything she wanted in material possessions because Arturo was generous, but she felt they were gradually but surely drifting apart to the point of leading almost separate lives. His was work and work, hers was work and emptiness. Words of affection and love were rarely mentioned or were spoken in a perfunctory manner. Weeks would go by before a sexual encounter. *Am I still in love with him?* she wondered.

She decided the time had come for them to have a serious talk. She told him that her life had become lonely and empty and if not for her work rather boring. She talked about couples she knew who always did interesting things on weekends exploring some of the hundreds of islands.

He listened intently but then pointed out the dilemma of the private businessman as distinct from those in regular employment. Without hard work, they would not be where they were—successful and wealthy. He told her that he was happy she had raised the subject because what they needed were children to fill in her time and give more meaning to their life.

She protested strongly saying she could never reconcile pregnancy with her work and did not want to stay home all day long to bring up and look after children. He suggested bringing Miguel and Ramon to help with the store and the repairs if and when her pregnancy became advanced, but she recoiled in horror. "You don't know Miguel as I do. I'm very fond of him, but I wouldn't put it beyond him to try to extract a high price for his services."

Arturo fell silent. He felt defeated. Didi was a bit surprised at her reaction to her family. Over the years, she had been sending them with Arturo's knowledge and approval a few thousand pesos on important occasions, but she felt more comfortable with them far away. She felt jealous of her success and did not want other members of the family to share it. More than that, in her soul, she did not wish to be identified with her brothers. She had become a relatively modern and a rather glamorous city girl, a far cry from the Mindanao girl she had been, whereas they were handymen from a rural town. The contrast with her would expose her origins, a thing she worked hard to conceal.

The discussion she had with Arturo while solving nothing

helped ease tensions for a while. For a week or two, he was more considerate and affectionate and joined her on a couple of occasions to the club, but then he gradually drifted back to his newer working and living habits.

In Search of Happiness

It was Sunday morning at the club. Didi, clad in a swimsuit, had stretched out on a reclining chair by the pool and was reading a magazine. It was warm and humid; the shade provided by the umbrella barely covered her.

"Excuse me, but are you Mrs. Fernandez?"

She raised her head and dropped her sunglasses down her nose to get a good look at the intruder. Facing her stood a young man grinning broadly with an apologetic expression on his face. She nodded in the affirmative.

"Forgive my intrusion. I know it is most inappropriate to ask you something at this time, but may I?" Without waiting for an answer, he grabbed a chair and sat beside her. "Our cook has been complaining bitterly. A food processor or a mixer—I forgot which, stopped working. I understand you have a business that takes care of such things. Can I please have your business address and phone number?"

He handed her a paper and a pen. She obliged. "The cook has been in the family for twenty years. If he is upset, we all suffer. I'll bring it to the store tomorrow," he said with a grin. "Are you planning to swim?"

"In a little while," she replied giving him a more probing look. His swimsuit revealed a muscular, fit, and well-tanned body. His face looked a tiny boyish, but despite the faint appearance of sweat over his brows, his slightly oversized nose, and his square jaw, he was a reasonably handsome young man.

"My name is Jaime by the way, but people call me Jimmy."

"I'm Dolores, but people call me Didi."

"I'm a university student. In a couple of years, hopefully I'll graduate in law."

"So you're planning on being a lawyer?"

"Oh no! That would be a hopeless proposition. If I ever attempted to defend a criminal, I'm sure they would put me in jail instead."

They laughed, and he continued. "I want to get into politics. A law degree is a good stepping-stone. Believe me, politics is the shortest possible route to power and wealth in this country."

For an hour, they chatted about everything and nothing. She found out that he came from the upper crust of Manila's society his father being a police general. He loved sports and was not particularly keen on academic achievements she gathered. It was obvious that he was a popular person at the club. Many people acknowledged his presence and waved at him while passing by. He told her he had been a member of the club for a long time as his family had joined it when he was a young boy.

"I noticed your coming to the club every Sunday often alone. Is there a Mr. Fernandez?"

"Rest assured there is."

"He's a very lucky man," Jaime said standing. "I enjoyed so much meeting you. I'll see you tomorrow."

Didi enjoyed their talk. It lifted her spirits. Talking

normally about other people's lives and aspirations brought some fresh air into her life; it was a change from her usual, daily preoccupation with work. Jimmy was an engaging and a courteous person she thought.

The following day, he showed up at the store. He looked bizarre walking with one hand behind his back. She greeted him with a smile.

"I checked with the cook again," he said. "The fool. Everything is working again properly after he fiddled with some wires he told me. I couldn't come empty-handed, so I brought you this." He swung his arm from behind his back and produced a beautiful bouquet of flowers.

"You shouldn't have!" She accepted it with a smile but with some embarrassment as other employees were discreetly watching.

"Didi, I have a problem I need to discuss with you. It relates to business. You may have gathered I'm hopeless in business. I'd really appreciate your advice. How about lunch at the Manila Hotel? Tomorrow perhaps?"

"I'm afraid that's impossible. I have so much to do."

"It's important and cannot wait till next Sunday. A strictly business lunch. Please don't say impossible, say maybe. I'll come tomorrow at one."

Before she could answer, he waved at her and left her clutching her bouquet. She spent the rest of the day and evening wondering what to do. He had aroused in her a feeling she had not felt in years, the feeling of excitement associated with baiting and luring a person of the opposite sex. He certainly was interested in her, perhaps not so much in her personality—she had hardly made any conversation with him—but most likely in her as a woman, a sensual type of exploration. Here he was faking an excuse to meet her, parading his body close to hers in a skimpy swimsuit, bringing her flowers, and inviting her for lunch. He certainly was younger than she was by a number of years, but that was never a barrier to physical attraction or desire. *Is there really a business problem he's facing, or is that yet another excuse? Should I accept his invitation?* Her inner feelings were urging her to do so. After all, a business lunch at the Manila Hotel would be innocent enough. For decades, that hotel has been the symbol of old-fashioned elegance patronized mainly by Filipinos high up in the social ladder. *Why not?* After all, he was not a dull person, rather handsome and presentable with good family connections that might come in handy someday. It would be a nice change and would break the monotony of having lunch alone at home. How could anyone possibly fault her for going to a business lunch? She picked up the phone and with a businesslike manner signaled her approval for that meeting as she called it.

When he showed up the following day in his blue BMW, she had him wait a good fifteen minutes while she finished some paperwork. After a brief disappearance to freshen up her makeup, she was ready to leave. He did not expect any apology for the delay, and none was offered.

"With the traffic at this hour, I hope we won't be late for our reservation," he told her after going through the third consecutive red light. Noting the perplexed feeling on her face, he added, "Policemen don't bother me anymore. They know I'm the unrepentant son of a general."

As they sat down for their lunch, Didi looked at him again. He was definitely good looking, perhaps five or six years younger than she was. "So what's the business problem you wanted to discuss?" she asked.

"I never discuss problems except after dessert, so why don't we talk about you? Do you play any sports or do physical fitness workouts?"

"Me? No!" She was startled.

"Impossible. I've been watching you at the club. How do you keep your body in such a magnificent shape?"

She blushed and did not respond. She felt like throwing the question back at him. If anything, his body was so fit that he looked like a professional athlete.

"I'm not trying to flirt with you, Didi. I'm just stating a fact. How could I flirt with you? You're married. I respect that. I concede defeat."

Didi was not entirely insensible to his overtures. They were music to her ears. It would be fun to hear more. For the next half an hour or so, they talked and laughed as she repeatedly fended off or pretended to ignore his compliments.

"Well, we're now having dessert, so what's your business problem?" Didi asked at last.

"I didn't say I had a business problem. I'm sure I said I had a problem I wanted to discuss over a business lunch. My problem is this. As you are married, I have to try the next best thing—find a girl like you. If ever I did, I would not be single for a day. I have to confess. I have a terrible desire to want to see you every day, not just Sundays. Why not? We enjoy each other's company, or at least I believe you enjoy mine as much as I enjoy yours."

She did not respond. Her smile dried up. She made a move to leave.

"Did I offend you?" he asked while opening the car door for her. "If you accept my proposal, I promise I won't go through red lights anymore."

They laughed.

"I'm surprised at you. What could possibly come from nurturing a relationship here? I enjoyed talking to you, but that's all. I have a husband you know."

"Are you in love with him?"

She did not respond.

"You give me some hope then."

He rang her the following day.

"I hit on a splendid idea. You bring your swimsuit tomorrow. We'll go for a swim and lunch at the club. What do you say?"

The idea appealed to her. It would certainly be refreshing to have a dip in the pool at high noon in the hot, muggy weather. Besides, the club served decent light meals that could break the monotony of daily home cooking. She had never been to the club on weekdays. Most probably it would be much less crowded she thought. But she said, "No, Jimmy."

"Well then, after tomorrow?"

"Maybe," she said with some hesitation and in a mischievous tone surprising herself with her boldness.

Two days later, she drove to the club. Having a dip in the pool in that heat was surely refreshing. She dried herself and looked at his body.

"I caught you looking at me. What you see is what you get," said Jimmy with a grin.

"I wasn't looking at all. You're too conceited."

"OK then, I have to admit I was looking at you, and what I see I cannot get."

She responded with a faint smile that was not all that innocent.

"You're not a regular here like me. You could get badly burned. Let me rub some sunscreen on you."

"No thanks, I can do that myself."

She rubbed some sunscreen over her body, lay facedown, and casually handed him the cream tube. "OK, you can do my back."

He sat beside her and began to slowly massage her back. She looked and spotted a movement of his organ under his swimsuit. It was not far from her mouth. She felt excited. It would have been wonderful if she had allowed him to massage all her body. But then reason prevailed. She needed to put an end to her fantasies. "That's fine. Thank you," she said while turning around.

He gave her a brief "I want you" look while waving to the waiter.

A leisurely lunch followed, and as they left, he persuaded her to repeat this encounter perhaps daily.

Three days later over lunch, he told her that he was moving out of the family home. He had seen an apartment he liked and wanted her to see it and give him her opinion on his renting or buying it. "It's on our way. It will take only a few minutes."

It was a small but tastefully furnished apartment. As she admired it moving from one room to the next, he suddenly took her in his arms. She tried to push him away, but he refused to be put off. She found her resistance weakening as he kissed her passionately. She yearned for affection. *What the hell*, she thought. Arthur had once relayed to her a quotation from Oscar Wilde: "The best way to get rid of a temptation is to yield to it." *Why not yield now and enjoy it?* She felt too young to have her desires tucked away in the name of a sterile marriage. She needed affection, love, and sexual fulfillment. This was exciting. She felt like a teenager, and he was a young and desirable partner, a young stud. She could try it once, give herself and her body a break from the monotonous, hectic, and empty life she had been leading. *Yield to the desire,* a voice inside her egged her on. *Nobody will know.*

With only a token resistance, she let him undress her while she slowly undressed him feeling every part she exposed from the hair on his chest to his excited organ that would soon tie them together. She felt his hands caressing her breasts and his thighs hugging hers. Soon, he dominated her in bed feverishly making love. Didi felt her body throbbing. She let out loud sighs. She was so relaxed and happy that she rewarded him with a hug and a passing kiss as she climbed over him to get out of bed.

"Wait. Let's do it again!"

"I can't. I have got to get back to work."

That evening, she wondered whether she should pursue further that exciting adventure or put an immediate end to it, *But how and why?* she wondered. When Arturo showed up late that evening tired and in his usual pensive mood, he did not as much give her a kiss or utter a word of affection. She felt then that he had made the decision for her.

Over the next month, Didi and Jimmy met about twice a week for a swim, a quick lunch, and a visit to his apartment. During the second month, however, things cooled a bit. They saw each other less frequently; while she enjoyed their sexual encounters, theirs was a relationship based on infatuation rather than love. They were gradually running out of topics to discuss. Being younger, at times, he portrayed immature behavior; that was typical of some of the spoiled brats of Manila's high society. She came from a modest background but had struggled through life. Her working experience and interaction with clients had turned her into a more mature person for her age. She was also beginning to feel an increased sense of remorse toward Arturo though she liked to blame his indifference to her needs for what had happened.

Then came that fateful day. Didi was getting ready to go to the club one Sunday when Arturo stopped her. "We need to talk. Are you having an affair with that good-for-nothing fellow?" He was fuming as he held her by her shoulders.

"Let go of me! You're mad. I'm not having an affair with anybody. He's just a friend."

He tightened his grip on her shoulders. "Is he really? Tell me, did you go to bed with him? Just tell me the truth." His voice was rising and quivering with anger.

"I sometimes meet him at the club for lunch, but that's all."

"You still don't want to tell the truth. Here I am working day and night to give you the life you always wanted and how do you respond? You go behind my back for a good-for-nothing kid. What do you see in him except that he's some kind of a stud?"

"He's of no consequence. Can we change the subject?"

But Arturo would not be put off. "You were there on Friday. I heard about it. When I arrived at the club an hour later, the waiter told me you had left, but you didn't show up at the store until much later when he dropped you off. Where did you go?"

She felt trapped. "I'm not telling you, and even if I were

having an affair, I wouldn't tell you. I'm an adult, and I'm free to do whatever I like."

"What do you mean you're free to do whatever you like? You're my wife, and don't you forget it. Don't you ever treat me like an idiot who'd swallow everything!" He was shouting at the top of his voice, and his hands pressed her shoulders even harder. "If I ever see you again with that fellow, I'll break his neck and yours, and that won't be the end of the matter!"

"You just try it! He's the son of a police general. As for threatening me, you'd better be careful." She was now shouting at him. "You keep telling me I'm your wife! I'm sick and tired of this loveless marriage. You're married to your work. I was legally wed to Arturo Fernandez, and he's dead!" She was shivering with rage. "You're an impostor, Arthur. You married me using a fake identity, and don't you forget that. That could land you in jail for years. Don't you ever threaten me again or tell me what I should do or not do because I'm your wife."

He was stunned. That was pure and simple blackmail. She left in a huff slamming the door. She wanted to turn her rage on Jimmy as well. She found him at the club with a young girl; they were laughing and whispering to each other. He waved at her. She did not respond. He came over.

"What's the matter, Didi? Are you jealous?"

"Get lost!"

"Ah, well, it's over then. It was nice while it lasted." He shrugged and walked away.

That bastard! she thought. *He's found another girl and is showing off.* She wished she had dumped him first. He had certainly hurt her pride. *Never again, never,* she told herself.

Two weeks passed by with Arturo and Didi hardly addressing each other. They slept in separate beds "since we're not really married" he explained sarcastically. They were too proud to call a truce. Deep inside, she regretted calling him an impostor. She began to turn things over in her mind. He had gone through a lot for her—deserting his wife and children, obliterating his past identity, and living for weeks with the unpredictable Abu Sayyaf people. Furthermore, as he said, he worked so hard to give her a comfortable lifestyle and what did she reward him with? An affair with an immature and a conceited idiot.

True, he did neglect her needs somewhat, but maybe he had just overlooked them with all the pressing deadlines at work. When she married him, she thought that their strong bond would last forever, that he would continue to write her love notes and tell her almost daily how much he loved her and lived for her.

She thought that the passion of the lovemaking they had experienced in their early days together would also last for good. The more the days passed, the more she felt the strain of being estranged from him. This had to end. She reminisced about the old days. If only she could turn the clock back to the time when he was a loving, affectionate, and a caring husband. Never mind her wounded pride. She should take the first step to win him back.

"Arturo darling, can we please forget all this unpleasantness for your sake and mine? I'm truly sorry if I hurt you," she told him one day while placing her hand on his shoulder.

"Leave the darling out of it," he answered while taking her hand off his shoulder.

Two days later at work, he received a phone call.

"Mr. Fernandez, this is Purita. I hope you remember me. I bought the dishwasher from you last week. I'm afraid it's not working."

He remembered her—a woman in her thirties, good looking, a nice and lively person. Didi was out and he had arranged her purchase at the time.

"I'm sorry to hear that. What's wrong?"

"The soap compartment doesn't always open. Can you fix it?"

"We will look at it for sure."

"Look, Arturo," she said using his first name, "don't send me any of your boys. I want you to come in person. I have more faith in you. It's brand new as you know. Can you come today?"

"I'm afraid that's impossible. How about tomorrow morning at eleven? I have your address."

"That would be perfect."

The next day, Purita showed Arturo to the kitchen. He knelt on the floor beside the dishwasher and began to test the soap compartment. She stooped over him. Her long hair was touching his cheek. She asked innocently, "Did you find out what's wrong?" He looked up to answer her. The top button of her blouse had intentionally or unintentionally become undone, and he saw a good part of her breasts hanging over him.

"It looks all right to me. Maybe we should test run it for ten minutes or so."

She left him and returned with two gin and tonics. "Let's have a drink while waiting. Wouldn't that be awful if it works? I'd feel bad if I made you come for nothing."

"I am afraid I don't drink on the job," he said, but noting

the disapproval in her eyes, he took a sip to be polite. The machine worked all right. "That's it, then. I'm on my way. If it happens again, call me."

"Thank you so much, Arturo, for coming. I really appreciate it." To his surprise, she bent forward and planted a tiny kiss on his cheek.

The following morning, she rang again. "Arturo, this is Purita. It's not working again. Can you come today? I'm really desperate."

It was six when he got there. She showed him to the kitchen. "Arturo, I have to get ready as I'm going out, so I'll leave you to look at it alone. I'll be in that room. After you test it, can you please let me know?"

Ten minutes later, he knocked on her door. It was slightly ajar. She invited him in. It was her bedroom. She was sitting at her dressing table drying her hair, and she was clad in a short mini kimono that exposed her thighs.

"It's working perfectly well."

She ignored his remark. "Now look at this. My hair dryer's not working. What am I going to do?" she asked in a discouraged voice. She turned to face him and held the dryer for him to see. He came close, but before he could take the dryer, she wrapped her left hand around his waist and with her right hand pulled down his pants zipper. She pushed her hand in sighing with closed eyes. She undid his belt and pulled down his pants. She then stood pushing her bare thighs against his. He tried to take her in his arms, but she slipped away letting her kimono fall on the floor. She lay in bed clad in skimpy white underwear. "It's not the dryer, darling, it's me who needs fixing," she said stretching her hands to welcome him.

When he left an hour later, he felt relaxed. He had not made love for a couple of months or more, and Purita had at least momentarily reduced the tension that had been building in him as a result of his strained relation with Didi.

Two days later, she phoned. "Arturo darling, it's me, Purita. I need fixing. Six tonight."

Before he could respond, she hung up. He showed up at her apartment excited about a repeat experience. But then three days passed without a call. He waited two more days. He was struggling with his thoughts. Should he pursue Purita? His wife seemed to be having an affair and had even gone to the extent of blackmailing him. She hurt him badly, and he wanted to get even with her. After some hesitation, he decided to phone. A man answered the phone. He heard him say, "It's for you, darling."

She came on the line. "Thank you for calling, Mr. Fernandez. All the machines are now working well. I'll call you if I need you again." She hung up.

Arturo could not understand what had gone wrong. It never occurred to him that there were a good number of normal people, men and women alike, married and single, who enjoyed a sexual adventure here and there without commitments or obligations.

Two weeks passed. The rainy season was in full swing. Arturo had parked near the store and with his umbrella wide open and dripping dashed into the store. He noticed two people deep in discussion with Didi. He gave them a cursory glance, but then he froze, turned, and dashed out as quickly as he could. One of the two was Rony. *What on earth brought him to this particular store?* he wondered. For the past five years, he had dreaded this encounter, but the chances of it happening in a city of over 10 million like Manila was infinitesimal, and he had taken comfort in that.

He was sure Rony had not noticed him, *But what if he did? How could I possibly explain my fake death? What if they denounce me to the police?* The news would certainly get back to his family. Janet and Mary would feel cheated and humiliated as would Lesley. How could he have been so foolish and so naïve to get duped into that scheme from which there was no way out? *There's no such thing as a perfect murder or a perfect disappearance for that matter. Was it worth it?*

His thoughts turned to Didi. How could he ever forgive her for being unfaithful after all he had gone through for her? To be fair, she had warned him some time earlier that all was not well in their marriage, but he had taken that lightly and dismissed it casually. They had been a great team, and she had contributed enormously to the success of the business. Like him, she too had changed. He missed the early days of courtship and marriage, and now that he was alienated from her, he missed these days much more. Deep inside, he was still fond of her, in fact very fond of her. He missed her affection and having her beside him in bed. *That whore Purita doesn't measure up one bit to Didi. How did I allow myself to be dragged into this affair only to be so unceremoniously dumped?* Arthur could not think straight. His life was a mess. He needed to get away from it all and think things over. When he told Didi he was going away for a couple of days, she simply shrugged.

9

Settling the Score

Didi sat in the living room reading a book, but she could not concentrate. It was Sunday evening. She had not gone to the club that day. She wanted to avoid seeing Jimmy, whom she felt had used and humiliated her.

At church that morning, she confessed and took communion. Arturo had been gone for three days. The house was empty. It being the maid's day off, she was alone. She wondered where Arturo could have gone. He had rarely if ever taken a vacation. *Is he trying to get even with me by taking another woman on a trip?*

She went over their last argument. True, he did neglect her needs, but did that justify a breakdown in their marriage? And where would she go or what would she do if that happened? Above all, her biggest regret was her threat to reveal his true identity. In fact, she regretted it almost immediately after she had said it, but she was too angry and too proud at the time to apologize. Almost a month had passed since then. Her discreet overture for reconciliation on a couple of occasions had borne no fruit. Arturo appeared uninterested, distant, and aloof. She was emotionally worn out. She had to find a way to ease the tension if reconciliation was improbable. She heard the front door open. *It must be Arturo.*

A few minutes later, he showed up in the living room with two gin and tonics. He gave her one and sat. It took him a few minutes to break the silence. "I needed to get away to think clearly," he said. "I went to Cebu."

"Cebu!"

"Yes, Cebu, the city of love as you called it. I stayed at the same hotel where we stayed eight years ago, walked the same streets, ate at the same restaurants. I even had dinner at the same table in the hotel where we went for the New Year's Eve party. I thought of the joy we experienced at the time. I asked myself what had happened to us. We were carefree and happy in those days." Didi tried to intervene, but he waved her off. "Please hear me to the end. I began to reason with myself by apportioning blame. I blamed you for everything. How could you have betrayed me? I was furious. I remained in this state for almost half a day.

"Then I reminisced about our early encounters in Mindanao, our walks, the notes I wrote you, and the many sleepless nights I spent thinking of you. I then recalled our adventure, my premature death and resurrection, the long days and weeks I spent at the Abu Sayyaf hideouts thinking of our forthcoming encounter but also of my family back home, the many doubts and fears I had then.

"I remembered how it was when we met again at Cebu, our wedding, the honeymoon, and that Christmas vacation. At the time, I never thought it possible for anybody to be happier than we were."

He put his glass down and gazed at her. Her eyes were swelling with tears. "We were poor, but I thought we doted on each other. We went on to build something together, and we succeeded. We assumed that happiness would automatically follow, but it didn't. The more successful I became, the more I wanted. Success became an end in itself.

"Wasn't I to blame as well for getting sucked in the whirlpool of work and taking you for granted? I asked myself why I should continue with this sterile argument about whose fault it was. What are we to do now? Where do we go from here? The answer came back to me quite clearly. What I really wanted was to turn the clock back, to relive those happy days we shared. If this cannot happen, maybe we should end our marriage. I'd live on past memories always remembering the happy times we shared together.

"During the last few weeks in particular, we've had many heated discussions. I probably said awful things to you as well. This I sincerely regret and ask for forgiveness. If you want a divorce, we can discuss the arrangemen—"

She rushed to hug him tears rolling down her cheek. "Arturo darling, it's I who should ask for forgiveness. I'd been so selfish and foolish. I betrayed you after all that you went through for me."

"There's nothing to forgive, Didi," he said stroking her hair. "I too had my little adventure. You see, the score is even."

"You, Arturo?" she asked in disbelief.

"Yes, Didi, a brief encounter with a woman, and believe me, it didn't bring me happiness. Did your adventure leave you happier person?"

She shook her head.

"While in Cebu, I made several decisions. I'll reveal them to you in due course. Do you trust my judgment, Didi?" When she nodded in the affirmative, he continued. "I need to go to England in two or three months. Can you manage without me for a few days?" She nodded again. "Then I want you to join me in London. We'll spend two weeks there on holiday."

"Oh Arturo! London! That would be wonderful! But what about the store?"

"I'm calling Miguel. I want him and Ramon to join us in Manila."

That startled her. "Miguel and Ramon? Here? To do what?"

"Miguel will help you in the store. He has a good, outgoing personality. He'll make a good salesman. I'll tell him to always wear a tie and be presentable, but you'll have to train him. I want him to relieve you at least partly from the daily pressures. Ramon will work with me on repairs. He's quite handy you know. I'll train him.

"I've also decided not to work weekends and always have our meals together, but that's not all. Guess where we're going next weekend? To Cebu with no more than a few thousand pesos in our pockets. I want to relive our Cebu days."

"Oh Arturo, I think I'm falling in love with you all over again," she said wiping her tears.

"In this case, may I regain my place beside you?"

Before she could even nod, he carried her to bed.

Two days later, he reported to her that Miguel was eager to come. His garage was not bringing in much income, and since he was married and had a two-year-old girl, he welcomed the opportunity to better his earnings. Ramon had agreed as well.

"Unfortunately, your mother refuses to join them. She says it's too late for her to leave familiar surroundings and start new friendships in Manila. She'll occasionally come to visit.

I offered to have Miguel and his family and Ramon stay with us for a month or so until they find suitable accommodations. I'll pay them a minimum salary. If after a couple of months we're satisfied with their performance, I'll sell them ten percent of the business at a preferential price they can pay off in installments. I want them to feel that they own part of this business and put in it all their energy and effort."

When Miguel and family arrived three weeks later, contrary to her apprehension, their presence introduced a breath of fresh air into Didi's life. She took Miguel's wife, a simple and sweet girl, on several shopping sprees showing her Manila. She became very fond of her baby niece spending most of her spare time playing with her and showering her with affection and toys.

Lesley was surprised to find a letter waiting for her from the Philippines. She thought she recognized the handwriting. She opened it with trembling hands and glanced quickly at the signature. Her heart skipped a beat. It was signed Arthur.

Dear Les,

I do apologize if this letter comes to you as a rude surprise. For contrary to what you have been led to believe, I am alive and well. It would take too long to explain to you what happened. When I left you, it never occurred to me in my wildest dreams that I would be deserting you and the girls. Alas, I have succumbed to the style of life in this country. For years now, I have also been living with a companion. We are happy together. I thought of you and our girls on many occasions. I want to see you and get your news firsthand, and above all, I want to make amends if that is at all possible for the pain and anguish I must have caused you.

Can we meet for dinner in London on Saturday, April 20? I have reserved two rooms at the Cavendish Hotel. It is next door to Fortnum and Mason I am told. You will have your own room. After our talk, we can decide when and how I will meet the girls. Please write immediately to confirm our get-together. I pray in my heart that you will find it possible to forgive me, for until you do, I will not forgive myself.

My love to you, Mary, and Janet. I am so anxious to see you all.

Yours
Arthur

Lesley read the letter again and again. She could not believe it. She buried her face in her hands and started to sob. Then a wave of anger overcame her. *That rotten bastard! What we went through after his presumed death! Did he desert us for the Filipina he mentioned? It can't be true!* she thought. He was such a decent person and a loving father. For the time being, she would not subject her girls to this, at least not until she heard his story. *The guts he has to ask for forgiveness! And the amends he mentions—What sort of amends?*

She had so many questions. Maybe she should be patient until they meet. What about David? She was happy with him. Was she going to dump him for an undeserving husband and father? She should discuss this letter with David at once. He would give her the best advice. She paced the floor waiting impatiently for him to return from the office.

Arturo waited anxiously for a reply. It arrived two weeks later.

Dear Arthur,

Needless to say, I was utterly surprised to receive your letter but relieved to know that you are alive after all. The date you suggested for our meeting suits me fine. I will probably arrive at the hotel around 5:00 p.m.

I went through a very hard time after your presumed death. I cannot understand the reasons that led the fine person you were to desert his family. Until I hear your part of the story, it may be difficult to talk about forgetting or forgiving. I noted that you have a companion. Lately, I too have met a person with whom I have found comfort and strength. David is a wonderful man, and he has been good to the girls. I shared your letter with him as we had some decisions to make. I wanted him to accompany me to London, but he said it would be best if you and I met alone at first.

For reasons best explained when we meet, I have not revealed your letter to Mary and Janet.

I too would like to discuss the future.

Yours
Les

They met at six at the bar of the Cavendish Hotel. Arthur did not know how to greet her. She allowed him a kiss on the cheek. He looked at her. She had put on some weight but still wore no makeup. "You haven't changed much," he said. "Give me all yours and the girls' news. I have ten years to catch up on."

"Why don't you start? How did this happen? I mean, the false report of your death?"

"I'll tell you later. Go on with your news."

"I received a letter from the priest in the Philippines. His name escapes me."

"Fr. Ramos."

"That's right. He announced your death. What a terrible shock to us all that was. The girls went to pieces, and I cried a lot and felt helpless and lost. The priest said that he buried you there but was awaiting instructions in case I wished to have you exhumed and reburied here. I figured that would cost upward of forty-five hundred pounds. I couldn't afford it at the time what with raising two children and the like and without your income, but I vowed that one day I'd bring you home."

"You don't have to worry about that now."

"I organized a memorial service for you, and Fr. Timothy said very nice things about you. I kept your belongings for a year in your cupboard not wanting to part with them. My biggest problem was making both ends meet. My salary is not much, as you know, and prices have gone up considerably since you left, but at least I was able to withdraw some of our savings at Barclays. David ironed things out for me. He works there. I often went to him for advice, and he was always most obliging."

"I'm honestly and truly sorry to have caused you all this suffering. I feel awful. Believe me, I thought of you all so often, but I couldn't bring myself to contact you for reasons I'll explain later, but please, Les, go on. Tell me about the girls. I'm so anxious to hear their news and to see them."

"They're very well, popular, have a good circle of friends,

and now as teenagers, they're coping with their changing emotions and feelings the best they can. Janet is growing up to be a composed, self-assured, fine person. Mary is more of a dreamer. Both are doing well at school, in fact very well. They're university material. Janet is at the Faculty of Arts and Mary is studying music. Here. I brought you their pictures."

Arthur looked long at the pictures and said pensively, "You didn't tell them I was back? I really would love to see them."

"When you left, they talked a lot about you. They told their friends about your whereabouts and achievements. They were really proud of you, Arthur. When the news of your death came, they took it to heart. They cried a lot and were emotionally upset for months. Gradually, they began to get over it, but they always put you on a pedestal. David's presence was reassuring for them.

"In your letter, you mentioned another woman. You haven't yet told me what happened, but since your letter arrived, I suspected that you left us for her. I then thought that if I told them that their father had deserted them to be with another woman, they would turn dead against you and perhaps not want to even see you. These things are not totally comprehensible to children. There is at first the feeling that they can easily be tossed away by a person they loved so much and for no fault of their own. Then there's the humility they'll have to go through when word gets around to their friends. I thought it better to save them all that, that is, until we met and discussed it. What do you think? The choice is really between being remembered always as a loving and an accomplished father or risk hurting them and yourself if they turn against you."

"I guess you're right, Les. Maybe it's better to leave things as they stand for now. However, from now on, I want to cover all their school expenses. They need not know about that. I want to set up a trust fund of twenty thousand pounds in their name. Each will have the right to half the money with interest when she becomes twenty-five or marries. I want them to have some financial independence when they start out. You can always tell them the money was left to them in my will."

"Arthur, that certainly will be a great help. They'll certainly appreciate it."

"Tell me about you, Les. What's the extent of your relationship with David?"

"David's a very nice and steady man. He's a widower. His wife died of cancer a year before you—Sorry! Before your supposed death. At first, David invited me for tea and later for a drink at the pub. You'd been presumed dead for two and a half years, a respectable period of time for us to be seen together in public. We went out occasionally at first and then regularly.

"One day, he suggested we spend our weekends together at his house. I hesitated a lot. The fact was that we were lonely and felt it most on weekends, and we enjoyed each other's company. I consulted the girls, and then I accepted. A few months later, we decided to live together. He moved into our house and helped support the family. The girls are quite fond of him. When they were teenagers, it was difficult at times to cope with them alone. They needed the steady hand of a father." She looked at him and said apologetically, "I'm sorry, Arthur. Things would have been very different if I'd known you were alive."

"I understand, Les, and I'm delighted for you. I wronged you all along. What are your plans now?"

"Well, Barclays is closing its branch where David works. They think highly of him and offered him a transfer to Southampton next September."

"Will he take the offer?"

"He's elated with the news and is very happy. He wants me to go with him … as his wife. Three months ago, he proposed."

"Did you accept? You love him, Les, don't you?"

She nodded. "Yes. I accepted to marry him and accepted the move to Southampton, and the girls were happy too, but there were hurdles to overcome even before your letter arrived."

"What hurdles?"

"Before we could get married, the civil authorities and the church wanted your death certificate. Six months after your disappearance, Fr. Ramos sent me what seemed like the certificate they wanted. I kept it in a box for years not knowing what to do with it. When I showed it to the authorities, they said it was not recognized in England, so we went to see a solicitor."

"What did he say?" Arthur could hardly conceal his excitement.

"He said that what we had was a police report, not a death certificate, that to obtain the certificate, he would have to contact a lawyer in Manila who in turn would contact another in the district where your accident took place. He didn't have such contacts but would make inquiries and get back to me. The certificate would then have to be certified by the British Consulate in Manila before it could be authenticated and registered here.

"We needed the certificate for another reason as well. If we were to move to Southampton, we'd sell the house, which is in your and my names. Again, that could not be done without your death certificate. Your letter then arrived and changed everything. I phoned the solicitor and told him to drop the case.

"You asked about our plans. Well, they really depend on yours and what you have to tell me. Are you thinking of reconciliation and under what terms? How could I be certain that you wouldn't leave again? And how could I drop David? Would that be fair?"

Arthur was not particularly listening to her. He was too excited.

"Les, do you realize what you just told me? This means that according to British law, I'm still alive. How wonderful!" That drew a blank from her. "Of course it wouldn't be fair to David. Believe me, I want to make it up to you in every possible way. Let's go for dinner."

Lesley wondered what he had in mind. She was determined to stick to her guns and get a fair deal. At the same time, she did not want to jeopardize her chances for a new married life with David, nor did she want to let Arthur off the hook so lightly. But she wanted to listen to his side of the story before she passed judgment.

They ordered a rack of lamb with roast potatoes with a bottle of Gevrey-Chambertin red wine. He had hardly lifted his glass to toast her when she asked him, "Now tell me, how did this accident take place? If it wasn't you, who was the person killed? Tell me about your companion, how you've lived since I last heard from you. And what are you doing at present? Are you teaching somewhere? I have so many questions."

Arthur collected his thoughts. He wanted to be frank with her and yet not necessarily divulge all unnecessary details. Every person has his own secret corner where he hides some of his inner feelings even from his closest partner. "If I hadn't contacted you earlier, it was because I lacked the courage. I thought about this encounter a great deal. Finally, I couldn't live with my conscience any longer. You guessed right. I loved the Philippines, and I succumbed to the charm of Didi, my companion, the first time I saw her.

"Don't ask me why or how. It's always difficult to find rational answers to emotional issues. Contrary to what you may think, she didn't try to seduce me. In fact, it took her a long time to … to love me. She comes from a modest background but is a delightful person and has been a great help to me in building my own business, maintenance and repair of household appliances." He did not tell her about the store.

"We've done reasonably well, and her two brothers are now my partners. The first year in the country was very exciting. I felt like a missionary. I helped train many people and encouraged them to set up businesses. You know all that from my letters. When I met Didi and we got to know each other better, I wanted so much to start a new life with her doing what I had been preaching—setting up a business of my own. We both worked and still work hard at it.

"As for the man involved in the accident, I really don't know anything about him. A friend who knew my feelings toward Didi managed to make this sound like a case of mistaken identity. That way, I could start a new life with a new slate under an assumed name, the dead man's name. It worked at least for the authorities there, but there has always been a part of me that wanted to pull me back to my true identity. I also lived in fear of being discovered one day. If that ever happened, how could I explain this to the authorities but above all to you and the girls? I knew I had to tell the truth one day, and so I sat and wrote you that note. I was so relieved to get your answer and to learn about David."

Lesley listened to him intently all the while caressing her wine glass. "Nothing would have happened with David if we had been together. I don't know what happened to our marriage. I never thought it was so shaky that it could crumble so readily."

"I asked myself that same question many times, Les. The more I thought about it, the more I came to the same conclusion. What each one longs for all his life is to love and be loved, and yet love is so fragile. For it to survive, it has to be constantly nurtured. Some people often think of love as a means to getting married or to living together, and once they reach that end, they take it for granted that love will continue to blossom and grow. Nothing can be further from the truth.

"How many marriages have broken down or relations severed simply because love was put on the back burner leading to a stale or a routine life or preoccupation with success at work? In our case, I venture to say that we're both to blame, and certainly I more than you. We allowed ourselves to live a sheltered life that centered on our work, going to church, TV, and raising children. Our emotions were subdued. When did I ever give you flowers, take you dancing, or drive you on weekends around the country or to the continent?

"When we parted, the passion in us had long been extinguished. We both became vulnerable. Meeting Didi and David fanned in us the fire of desire. The prospect of pursuing and being pursued was exciting, and our lust for love was revived in an ardent, almost irresistible manner. It was not difficult to succumb."

Lesley listened to him closely. What he said seemed to make sense to her. She could not help feeling as she glanced at him that he was a changed man. He was no longer the timid person she had married. Gone were his earlier inhibitions. He was prepared to expose his inner feelings and discuss them. She had lived with him for ten years, but she had not seen him for another ten. Time had obliterated many details of their life together. Moreover, over the last five years, her emotional life has been taken over by David.

Arthur broke the silence. "Les, are you at all able to forgive me?"

"Arthur, you say I bear part of the blame too. How could I? You were the man in the family. You should have taken the lead in correcting whatever you saw wrong in our marriage. What can be more humiliating to a married woman than to know her husband left her high and dry for another woman? Don't talk to me about forgiveness. What would have happened to me if I hadn't met David? Did you think about it, or are you too self-centered to have ever bothered to do so?"

Arthur interrupted with a slight wave of his hand as a sign of resignation. "You have every right to be angry. I'm entirely to blame. I've been dreading this encounter for years. Can we stop rehashing the past and start talking about the future?" He raised his glass, but she did not reciprocate.

"What about the future? What do you have in mind?"

"You cannot marry David because I'm alive, and I can't marry Didi because I'm dead at least in the eyes of the Philippines authorities. Since coming to London, I made some inquiries and was given the name of a good lawyer. I booked a tentative appointment with him for Tuesday morning. I am to confirm it tomorrow morning as I didn't know how our discussion would go. If it's OK with you, we can start our divorce proceedings immediately. Obviously, I will plead to be the guilty party, will admit to deserting you, and to adultery. If there is no contest on your part, the process shouldn't be too lengthy. We'll discuss the terms in a minute, but is this agreeable to you?"

She nodded reluctantly but approvingly.

"As we'll be getting a civil divorce, yours and my marriage, alas, will have to be civil as well, no Catholic church weddings. I don't mind, and I hope you don't mind either."

She did not respond.

"Can you get away and join me in London on Tuesday? You can return the same day. If you wish to come a day earlier or stay a day longer, I'll be happy to make arrangements with the hotel."

"No, I'll come and return the same day."

"How much do you reckon our house is worth?"

"It can probably fetch a hundred thousand pounds."

"Right. I want to sign my share over to you. In addition, I'll transfer to you fifty thousand pounds to atone for my sins."

"I must admit that's a generous offer. Of course, I don't really know how much you're worth."

"In pesos, I'm a millionaire, but in Her Majesty's currency, I'm afraid that my savings are not much more than an average bloke. As for the sum I intend to give you, I reached this calculation as follows. I figured out that for the last several years, I should have contributed forty thousand or thereabouts to your coffers. I then asked myself, 'How

GEORGE KANAWATY

could I possibly give her less than ten thousand as a wedding present?'"

"It is sweet of you, Arthur, to say that."

He stretched his hand to her. "Friends?"

She took his hand. "Friends," she replied.

"There's one issue that's very important to me. I don't want to lose touch with the girls even if you say I am better off not meeting them. Can you keep me posted every few weeks about their progress and their news, progress at school, university, boyfriends, and so on?"

"I will."

"Les, why don't you bring David with you and stay over? I'd like to meet him. Didi arrives Tuesday. We can do our chores with the lawyer that morning leaving her to rest. All four of us can then have dinner later. You should meet her. I want you to."

"I really don't want to meet her, though maybe you should meet David."

"Please, Les."

"All right. I'll force myself to do so if it pleases you. It would be difficult for us to take more than a day off. How about tea at four? That way, David and I can take the evening train back. I'll check with him and confirm it by phone."

"Les, can you bring with you the police report issued in the Philippines regarding my death? You won't be needing it, will you?"

"Certainly not. You're very much alive. I'll bring it."

He walked her to her room but could not get himself to do so arm in arm; both felt estranged from each other. With a goodnight kiss on the cheek, Arthur left her and was feeling happy and content. That dreaded meeting had gone well. It had surpassed his expectations. He could put his worries behind him. The discussion had gone on without too much recrimination, and more important, the possibility of his reclaiming his identity appeared attainable. That joyful prospect kept him awake for hours.

Tuesday promised to be a hectic day. Arthur showed up at Heathrow before five in the morning. His heart skipped a beat when he saw Didi passing through the exit gate. It was as if he had not seen her in years. They hugged and kissed several times. He asked her about the flight and whether she was able to sleep on the plane. She was too excited to do so she said. Coming to Europe was a dream she had held ever since she was a girl.

"So what sort of mischief have you been doing behind my back in London?" she asked.

"I'm not telling you everything. I'll take you to our hotel and leave you there to rest while I attend to some business, but this afternoon, we'll have tea with Lesley."

"Lesley! Your former? I mean your wife?"

"Yes, I want you to meet. She's bringing David, her companion."

"She has a companion?"

"Yes. Apparently a fine man."

"Are you sure this is a good idea?"

"I'm sure, trust me. We had a long talk and agreed amiably to a divorce. And in a few hours, we may be starting the procedure for it."

"Oh Arturo, you're full of surprises! Stop! I can't take any more excitement."

He kissed her, helped her into bed, wished her a nice rest, and slipped out.

At the lawyer's, he set up the trust fund for Janet and Mary, made the arrangements for a divorce settlement, which involved covering the girls' scholastic expenses, a £50,000 cash settlement, and his share of the house. The lawyer told him and Lesley that given his admission of guilt and the no contest from Lesley, the procedure could be completed in four to six months.

When the four met for tea that afternoon, they avoided talking about the subject that had brought them together. Instead, Lesley and David inquired about life in the Philippines, and Arthur was keen on getting news of his hometown. It all went amiably, and before they knew it, the time had come for them to part. As they did so, Lesley fell behind and pulled Arthur by the arm. "She's a nice girl, Arthur, and quite attractive too," she whispered. "Congratulations. I didn't think I'd like her, but I do."

"And I like David. He's a fine man and will make a perfect husband. I wish you both the best."

The four of them kissed before going their ways.

"Didi," he said, "let's wander the streets and go for an early dinner and an early night. Tomorrow will be another day. I want you to wear something nice in the evening as I'm taking you to a nice place for dinner."

Arthur had booked a room at the Cadogan Hotel, one of London's smaller but warm and elegant hotels. It was within walking distance of Harrods. They woke up late, had breakfast, and headed to Harrods. She was overcome by the store, the food hall, the Egyptian room, the various snack bars and restaurants, the almost unlimited variety of everything from stationery to clothes to kitchen and bathroom equipment. They spent some time at the appliances department comparing makes and prices and returned to their hotel that afternoon with tired feet and several shopping bags. She told him that she could spend days in that store, and he warned her that there were several other stores perhaps not as big but well worth visits as well.

The next evening, he took her to the dining room of the London Regent Hotel. He ordered a bottle of champagne while they were examining the menu.

"Arturo, this place is frightfully expensive by Manila's standards. Can we afford it?"

"It's expensive even by London standards but not by the standards of places of this caliber. At any rate, I have an ulterior motive for bringing you here."

She gave him an inquisitive look.

"Didi, will you marry me?"

"But we're already married. Are you still holding a grudge against me because I told you we weren't?"

"You were right. You were legally married to Arturo Fernandez. Now, it's Arthur Jones who's asking you to marry him. Will you accept to become Mrs. Jones instead?"

"Yes, Arturo … Sorry, yes, Arthur. I'll be so happy to marry you again if that's possible."

They raised their glasses. "To our everlasting happiness. I'm madly in love with you." He sent her a kiss across the table.

"And I adore you." She reciprocated with a kiss of her own.

He told her how he had learned from Lesley that as Arthur Jones, he was still very much alive in the United Kingdom as no death certificate had been issued or registered to that effect in his name. "Tearing this up would now be in order, don't you think?" He produced the Philippines police report on his death. Didi felt very happy—no more assumed names, no more worries, and the real Arthur Jones proposing to her.

"Didi, we have so much to look forward to. I want to really spoil you, but let's first discuss two problems. We'll get married here in the UK, but to do that, we'll need a certificate that you're single. I'm sure Miguel can help us as he did before. When you left Kipagah, you were single. With his contacts and a bit of greasing of the bureaucracy, I'm sure Miguel will face little problems getting that certificate."

She nodded. "There shouldn't be much of a problem I think."

"Second, we'll have our civil marriage here, but as a divorced man, we cannot have a Catholic wedding. On the other hand, if we convert to Protestantism, we can also get a church wedding. What do you think? I'm easy."

"I'd rather stay Catholic and live with you in sin," she said laughing. "What does it matter? We'll be man and wife in the eyes of the law, and maybe God will understand our plight and forgive us."

Armed with a guide to historic pubs, a map of the underground, a list of museums, and a theater guide, Arthur and Didi set out to discover London. They visited the Tower of London, Windsor Castle, and Westminster Abbey, and they shopped on Regent and Oxford Streets. They had drinks and snacks at historic pubs, and in the evening, they went to the theater whenever they could.

Arthur was eager to show her Wales. He rented a car, and they drove to Cardiff and passed through his hometown. He did not stop there; he just showed her the Swan Pub, where his father used to go, and passed his old house and the school where he'd once taught. He told her that the town owned its existence to the coal mine, and when the mine closed, things went downhill at first, but apart from some changes here and there such as new buildings, things looked familiar to him. In contrast, he had changed a lot. He could not think of himself living there again. It was a hypothetical question anyway since some people in town had attended his memorial service years earlier.

Arthur wanted to show Didi northern Wales with its national parks. He had heard of Snowdonia National Park but had never been there. He headed toward Swansea and skirted the city heading north. They passed many picturesque towns and villages, and they stopped at some inns for lunch and drinks on the way.

He parked the car, and they took the narrow-gauge railway to the top of Snowdon, the highest mountain in the UK, where a breathtaking view was there for them to enjoy. After a night at a National Trust hotel, they drove west the following day to the coastline of Merioneth and Lleyn, an area of sandy bays and rocky cliffs. There they sought a hotel for the night.

Like teenagers in love, they walked on the beach hand in hand smelling the fresh, salty breeze and picking up some shells. They talked about the differences between the UK and the Philippines.

The way back took them through Newport, Bristol, and the beautiful city of Bath, which they spent a couple of days exploring. Didi was overwhelmed by the beauty of nature in Wales and by the quaintness of the inns and guesthouses they stayed at or dined in. The fact that Arthur spoke Gaelic brought them an added sense of belonging and warmer hospitality.

When their two weeks were up, Arthur suggested extending their holiday by a week promising to take her to Stratford for a Shakespeare play. Didi did not need much persuasion. She loved the UK.

Arthur, who was discovering his own country at the same time as she was, had been turning a thought in his mind and wanted to discuss it with her. "Didi, what do you think about coming to live here for good? We can always go back to the Philippines to visit. There's so much to see in Europe."

"I'd love it, Arthur! But can we manage it financially? Things are quite expensive here."

"It shouldn't be too bad. We can sell the business to Miguel and Ramon or others and get our money over say a four-year period. We can sell our house in Manila. We have some savings, which we can invest. We won't be as comfortable as in Manila perhaps—no cook, no live-in servant—and money will not be readily coming in, and we'll be spending much more, so all in all, we may become poorer. But you know we were happiest when we were poor. Do you remember our early days in Cebu and Manila?"

"Arthur, we were happy not because we were poor but because we were embarking on an adventure and creating something. Our happiness decreased when we allowed our business venture to take over our lives. We've learned something, Arthur. Why don't we start a new business here? It would be so exciting!"

"What do you have in mind?"

"Can we open a store for sales and repair of appliances?"

"I doubt that will get us anywhere here. This is a different culture. People usually call manufacturers' agents for repairs, and it's difficult for small stores to compete with big department stores or agents' stores. On the other hand, there may be an opportunity in household maintenance including, say, gardens upkeep. I'll talk to some real estate agents."

"That's great, Arthur! Can I help in the future by answering the phone?" She had a mischievous look in her eyes.

"No, not again. You did it before and ended up running a whole store," he said laughing. "In this country, I don't need someone to answer the phone. I'll have a portable one."

"Maybe I can keep the accounts and do the paperwork."

"Done!"

"How exciting! Arthur, you're such an angel, and I'm a very lucky girl."

"Don't be so sure of yourself. You still have to trade the warm weather of Manila for a cold, wet, and at times depressing climate here. Besides, you may find people here to be less warm than those in Manila and perhaps rather aloof, but they don't mean it. They'll help you if you ask for help, but you must take the first step, and don't be shocked if you get a cool reception at first. People value their privacy here, yours and theirs. They'll allow friendships to develop up to the point they don't encroach on their privacy."

"Arthur, I love it here even if it is wet. We have two rainy seasons in Manila, have you forgotten? As for the rest, I'll do my best to fit in, I promise."

"Well then, we have to think of our honeymoon."

"A second honeymoon with the same man? That could be boring except if you come up with a brilliant idea," she said teasingly.

"I'm planning to take you to Paris and southern France—Nice, Cannes, or Saint-Tropez, or maybe all three."

"Oh Arthur, I'm so excited! I can hardly wait for our wedding day."

"It's just a marriage, no wedding!" he reminded her. "Let's visit one or two real estate agents."

They selected a nice house in a quiet area of Wimbledon, where they could reach the center of London in forty minutes outside rush hours.

Six months later, Arthur and Didi got married in London.

"Our train leaves to Paris in four hours. What does my radiant bride want to do in the meantime?"

"There's one thing I want more than anything else in the world. Carry me to bed. I want to bring our children to life."

New Family Ties

When Andrew returned home from work that evening, he threw one glance at Janet and figured out something was wrong. He did not have to ask her; she was impatient to tell him.

"I saw the trust company today about my inheritance. These people are crooks. Can you imagine? They told me the balance of my account after deducting management fees was slightly less than twelve thousand pounds. How can that be? My father died thirteen years ago. He must have set up that trust before then. I expected seventeen to eighteen thousand pounds. I have a good mind to sue them."

"Let's have a whiskey and discuss this quietly."

Andrew returned with the drinks sat beside her and took her hands into his. "Did you discuss this balance with them?"

"Of course I did, and you know what they said? That the money came into their possession only three years ago."

"Maybe that's so."

"How can this be, Andrew? Would my father's ghost have decided all of a sudden to come out of the grave to set up the trust? This is ridiculous, unless ..."

"Unless?"

"You don't suppose mother tampered with our inheritance, do you?"

"Highly unlikely."

"I set an appointment for next week with the solicitor. I'm determined to follow this matter up. This money is ours, and we can use it. Of course if it is mother, I won't make a fuss. I told you all along that she didn't want me to rehash the past as she put it."

"Things will clear up next week. In the meantime, let's look at the papers and see what films are showing tonight."

Mr. Sykes, the solicitor, received Janet with the courtesy due to colleagues in the same profession. He was a much older man than she had imagined; he was bald with shaggy eyebrows and 1930s-style gold-rimmed glasses that hung precariously on the tip of his pointed nose. The leather chairs in his office were from another era, and his wooden desk was piled high with files.

Janet explained her predicament. The trust company was telling her that the funds had been deposited only three years earlier. She wanted to cross-check this information with him before deciding on her next move. Had it taken more than ten years to settle the estate?

He listened carefully as he leafed through a file on his desk. "Yes, I'm afraid this is correct. Here it is right in front of me. A trust fund was set up for the benefit of Janet and Mary Jones by Arthur Jones in 1991. It is signed, sealed, and registered."

"In 1991?" Janet exclaimed.

He continued to examine the file without noting the astonished look on Janet's face. "It's part of a divorce settlement, not an estate."

Janet's jaw dropped. "Divorce you say?"

"I hope I'm not betraying my clients' confidence, but surely you know that your father and mother were divorced in 1991."

"Yes of course," Janet said. "It's just that I lost touch with my father and knew of this trust only after my marriage."

"Quite."

"I would like to write and thank him. Do you by any chance have his address?"

Sykes examined the file once more before writing on a piece of paper the address of a certain Arthur Jones in Wimbledon.

When Janet left the office, she felt as if her legs would not support her. She could not think straight. *Could there be two Arthur Jones, one buried in Mindanao and another living in Wimbledon? How can Mother be widowed and then subsequently divorced from the same man?* She thought that Mrs. Diaz in Mindanao may not have been crazy after all when she said that Arturo was away, but why had she panicked when she found out that Janet was Arthur's daughter? Are Arturo and Arthur the same person? What was she trying to hide? Everybody was hiding something, above all, her mother. *If Arthur in Wimbledon is my real father, why has he been hiding, and where has he been all these years?*

The more Janet struggled to find answers, the more questions she raised. She needed to clear her thoughts with someone she could trust. She should speak to Andrew and Mary. Her sister was as concerned with this development as she was.

Back home, Janet collapsed in a chair. She needed a drink. For a good hour, she turned the events in her mind over and over. Was it really her father who was living in Wimbledon? It must be. Why would a stranger leave her and her sister money as part of a divorce settlement? Divorce! She could not believe it. Why should her mother hide the truth from her? Why did she persist in claiming that her father was dead and buried in some faraway country? She could not take the suspense any longer. She had to find out the truth. It was an impossible hour to reach Mary but probably a good time to phone Lesley.

"Mom! I went to see the solicitor today. He told me that you and Dad got a divorce three years ago. I couldn't believe it. Is that true?"

A silence prevailed on the other end of the line.

"Mom! Is Dad not really dead? I want the truth, Mom." Janet was quivering with anger.

Lesley's response was low as if it came from a distant planet. "I dreaded this moment for a long time. No, he's not dead."

"Why didn't you tell me? What were you trying to hide? You don't trust me? Why all this comedy of his being dead and buried many years ago? Tell me the truth. I have the right to know."

"I didn't know myself that he was alive until three years ago when he wrote me out of the blue. By that time, he had been involved with another companion and ... Well, there was David, so we agreed on an amicable divorce. The only other alternative would have been reconciliation, which both of us were reluctant to go through with for various reasons. I hesitated a great deal about telling you and Mary. I knew how much you loved your father and how hurt you would be if you knew he had cheated on us all. Besides, I felt humiliated at the time after learning that he left me for another woman, a Filipina girl."

"A Filipina girl? Is this what happened? But Mom, you could still have told me."

"If Andrew was fooling around with another woman, would you have told me, Janet? No. We have our pride. I decided to let things be. I felt that one day the truth would come out, but I didn't expect this to happen so soon. But now that it has, a big burden has been taken off my shoulders."

"But Mom! How can he desert us just because he fell for another woman? I just can't understand this."

"Well he did. He said that one cannot explain emotional behavior by rational thinking."

"This is incredible. What about that grave in Mindanao? I feel doubly cheated having gone to the Philippines especially to visit him."

"He said it was a case of mistaken identity. A friend there had arranged it. He didn't go into details."

"But that's terrible! As far as I'm concerned, I want nothing to do with him. It is as if I never had a father. I don't ever want to see him again."

"You do what you think is right, Janet. I understand how you feel. I had the same feeling when he wrote telling me he was alive. Then we met and sorted matters out, and I must say that now I feel more relaxed about the whole thing. I'm happy with David, and he's happy with his girl. Things turned out better than I'd expected. To be fair though, I have to tell you that he's paid for your education for the last several years."

"But it's not his money I wanted. I wanted fatherly love. He deserted me when I needed him most, during my teen years. I'm going to return his money. I don't want it."

"Don't be foolish, Janet. He's your father, and he owes it to you. Besides, I don't think his love for you and Mary has diminished. He made me promise to keep him posted as to your news."

"That's not good enough for me. Love is a two-way street. Who is this Filipina girl anyway?"

"Her name's Didi. They're married. I met her."

"You what?"

"She's a nice person, attractive, and much younger than he is. Very different from me I would say, but then your father is also a changed person. We all change with time I suppose."

"This alters nothing for me. I'll continue to resent him for what he did."

Now that she had learned the truth, Janet felt even more upset; she needed a breath of fresh air. Andrew was not due home for another four hours. She put on her coat and scarf and took her umbrella. She had no particular destination in mind. She just wanted to get out and lose herself in the crowds and distract her mind. She decided to go first to Mary's apartment. As she suspected, Mary was not there. She left her a note asking her for dinner. As an afterthought, she added "Come early. We have an important matter to discuss."

It was shortly after six when Mary showed up. She gave her sister a kiss. "I got your note. I'm starving. What are we having for dinner? And what's this important subject you want to discuss?"

"Andrew will be here any minute. We can talk about it then. Would you like a glass of sherry?"

"No thanks, but if you have an open bottle of red wine, I'll have a glass."

"No matter, Mary. We're opening a bottle tonight

anyway. We'll all need it. I'll get you a glass. Tell me about the academy."

"It's great, lots of hard work though. With the theoretical part and the performance part, it's really demanding, but I'm very happy. We're rehearsing for a concert next month. This will be my third time playing with the students there. Many concertgoers have no idea how much effort we put into rehearsing. Every conductor wants to mold us into his vision of how a particular piece should be interpreted. It's normal, I suppose, but as a result, we go through endless repetitions of almost every line of the score."

At this point, they heard the key turn in the door. "That's Andrew," Janet said.

Andrew greeted Mary warmly, kissed his wife, and settled down to a glass of red wine. Janet was anxious to relay to him and to her sister her news. She briefed them about her meeting with the solicitor and the telephone conversation with her mother.

Mary got quite emotional. "If Daddy's alive, I want to see him. Do you have his address?"

"How can you want to see him after what he did? I certainly never want to meet him. He's a cheat and a liar as far as I'm concerned. You do what you want, Mary. I want no part of it."

"Darling, you shouldn't be that harsh in your judgment. Whether you like it or not, he's still your father," Andrew said.

"I'm surprised at you, Andrew. How can you be so accommodating when he sent us on a witch hunt to lay flowers on an unknown man's grave and during our honeymoon of all times?"

"To be fair, Janet, he never asked you to do that or to go

to Mindanao. Even your mother tried to discourage you from going."

"So now it's my fault for trying to show my love for the father I knew? This discussion is getting nowhere." Tears of frustration were welling up in her eyes. *How can they not see the situation as I do?*

To diffuse the tension, Mary assured her sister that though now she knew of her father's whereabouts, she was not going to contact him in the immediate future. She wanted to think it over carefully. However, she had to admit that she had an ardent desire to meet the father she vaguely remembered.

When Arthur answered the doorbell, he stood transfixed before the figure in front of him. "Mary!" He unconsciously stretched his arms out to hug her before dropping them to his side.

"Daddy?" Mary asked in a probing tone.

"Come in! Come in! I can't believe it. I waited so long for this."

He hugged her very tightly retaining his tears. With his arm around her, he led her to the living room. Mary, overtaken by emotion, wiped her eyes.

"Let me introduce you. Mary, this is my wife, Didi, and that little fellow hanging onto his mother's dress is Edward. Didi, this is Mary of course."

Didi rushed over and gave Mary a kiss, and the boy followed giving Mary a beaming smile. "I'm so happy you came. Please sit," said Didi while holding Mary's hand.

Whatever apprehension Mary had had before coming dissipated. She had been made to feel so welcome already. She looked around her. The living room was tastefully furnished and tidy—beautiful paintings on the walls, Persian carpets on the floor, and lots of art objects from the Far East. "I hesitated before coming wondering whether I should call you beforehand, but then I decided to just drop in. I hope I'm not disturbing any plans you have. I won't stay long anyway."

"Nonsense! What could be more important than your being here, our being together? I hope you can stay long enough this and other times. We have to catch up on so much lost time. As for this evening's plans, this being the first Friday of the month, my clients and their friends are invited over here for wine and snacks. It was Didi's idea, and it's helped a great deal in building up a steadily growing clientele. Please Mary, stay for a drink. I'd love it if you could. People will start showing up in an hour or so, and the whole thing will last no more than an hour and a half. They are nice people. Do please stay."

"All right, I will, but Daddy, I have so many questions for you."

Didi excused herself saying she needed to get ready for their guests.

"Daddy, you recognized me right away yet you hadn't seen me since I was little. How's that possible?"

"Oh, no. I saw you a few times since I came back to England." He paused. "I suppose by now you must know the whole story. Otherwise, you wouldn't be here. Come. I want to show you something."

Taking her hand, he led her to a sideboard. To her surprise, she saw two framed photos—one of her holding her cello and the other of Janet and Andrew, their wedding picture. "I asked your mother for pictures of you as soon as

I came back and wanted the wedding picture as well. I was there you know," he added casually.

"You went to Janet's wedding?"

"Of course. I wouldn't have missed it. I went to the church and slipped out just before Janet and Andrew walked out. She looked absolutely radiant. As for you, Didi and I attended your two public performances."

"You did?"

"Yes, and I felt so proud of you. I had this terrible urge to go after the concert to kiss you and congratulate you. In each case, I pointed you out to the person sitting next to me telling him with some pride that you were my daughter."

"You did that!" She gave him a big hug.

"And now that we're together, nothing will separate us again."

"Tell me about your work. What are you doing now, and how is it going?"

"It is what I call property maintenance and management. I have an office, a full-time employee, and access to five others on a part-time basis. They include gardeners, painters, and the like. We started three years ago and are doing reasonably well. This wine we offer every first Friday of the month has generated lots of new business in addition to consolidating old contacts. I invite previous customers indicating that their friends are welcome. I also invite real estate agents. Possibly twenty people or so will show up tonight. It doesn't really cost much, and it builds a lot of goodwill."

"Are you happy, Daddy?"

"Didi is a wonderful and cheerful person."

"And quite attractive too I might add."

"We're very happy together, and when little Eddy arrived

on the scene two years ago, he brought us so much joy. Didi's father was Eduardo, so we decided to call him Edward. Of course, you and Janet have been missing from my life, but now here you are. Why didn't you bring Janet and Andrew with you?"

"I was last with Janet some two months ago when I went to her house for dinner, but we speak often on the phone. I was planning to go and see her this weekend."

"I suppose she knows about me."

Mary nodded. "I didn't tell her I was coming to see you. Actually, Janet is having a hard time. She just had a miscarriage. She's quite depressed."

"How awful! Nothing could be more painful. You know, on many occasions whenever I thought of the prospects of not seeing you both again, I felt so depressed. Do you suppose it's a good idea for me to go and see her?"

"Not now, Daddy. Give her some time."

Didi rejoined them well dressed and made up. "Everything's ready," she announced. "But before anybody comes, Mary, how about having lunch with us this weekend?"

"Thank you, but I'm planning on visiting Janet on Sunday," she replied shyly.

"Make it Saturday then. Please do come. I'll cook a Filipino meal for you, or would you rather have Chinese?"

"It's been wonderful to be here, but I don't really want to intrud—"

"I have a better idea," Didi said. "We can get the ingredients from London. Why don't I pick you up tomorrow morning? We can go shopping together. I'll show you some of the oriental stores, and then we can come back here and prepare the meal together."

"Splendid idea. Say yes, Mary, please," Arthur said.

"All right then. Thank you. I'd love that."

The doorbell rang, and the guests began to stream in. Arthur introduced his daughter around. Several people were impressed when they heard that Mary was studying at the Academy of St Martin-in-the-Fields. Every once in a while, Arthur would make the rounds refilling wine glasses. Didi moved from one group to another engaging everybody in conversation. People seemed to be enjoying themselves. Mary did as well. When the last of the guests slipped away, Mary asked her father if she would be invited to the next wine party.

"Most certainly," Arthur answered. "You have a standing invitation to all of them."

The following day proved to be an interesting experience for Mary. Didi took her around Soho in London. They moved from one oriental food store to another with Didi explaining the ingredients used in typical Filipino and Chinese cooking. They talked a lot. Didi asked her about the academy, her career aspirations, whether she had steady boyfriends. There were none at the moment, Mary replied.

In the short time she had known Didi, she had gotten to like her and her warm, outgoing, and cheerful personality. She could not conceive of her being her stepmother; Mary was only eight or nine years her senior she figured. She could very easily pass for a good friend. When they sat for tea before heading home, Mary felt at ease enough with her to inquire how she and her father had met.

"Arthur says he saw me first at church. I never noticed him, but then he rented the second floor of our house. He complained later saying I ignored him for a good part of two months, never giving him a chance for an overture. The truth is that I came from a modest background growing up in a rural town on the island of Mindanao, and there he was, a mature foreigner who appeared well off, ten years older than me, married with a family, who wanted to befriend me.

"It took me some time to get over my inhibitions, but once I did, I enjoyed his company. He was and still is one of the nicest, gentlest, and most affectionate persons I've ever met. Little did I know then that he had fallen for me. The last thing I wanted was to take him away from his wife and children. When he told me that he loved me, I tried to reason with him and with myself, but then I found myself gradually falling in love with him too. The rest you know. His determination overpowered my hesitancy and resistance. What he went through disguising himself as another person so that we could marry … You probably know by now that we were married under his assumed name at first.

"This experience can be judged differently by different people. Some may think of it as immoral, and others might tolerate it, but as far as I'm concerned, his ordeal created a strong bond that tied us together despite the usual ups and downs of married life.

"We talked a lot about you and Janet over the years. I felt I knew many things about you before we ever met. When we moved to England, your father continued to be torn between feelings of happiness and sadness. Here you were physically close to him yet beyond his reach. Your visit yesterday meant a lot to us. We should constantly keep in touch from now on, that is, if you're willing to accept me not as a stepmother but as a friend."

"Of course."

"Then let's go home and see what we can do with what we've bought."

It was a delightful day for Mary. She participated in preparing the meal; she found it distinctly different but very tasty. She enjoyed her father's frequent expressions of affection and spent a considerable time sitting on the floor with little Eddy playing with him with the toy she had brought him. She offered to babysit for them whenever that could be arranged.

Andrew had gone out to play tennis that Sunday morning, and Janet was happy to have Mary's company. They talked about various things before Mary broke the news. She knew how bitter Janet had turned against her father and decided to use restraint in her account.

"I visited Father yesterday."

"And so you did," Janet responded with indifference.

"They live in a nice house and have a two-year-old, Eddy."

"Here I am twenty-four with a two-year-old half-brother. How ridiculous."

"He's cute."

"You must have met his wife, my stepmother, I suppose."

"I liked her."

"So she charmed you the way she seduced my father."

Mary ignored the remark. "He misses you, Janet. He thought you might have come with me. He asked if he could come to see you, and I told him you weren't feeling well."

"You should have told him that I didn't want to see him."

"He had our pictures on the sideboard."

"He probably put them there to impress you."

"He didn't know I was coming. I dropped in without

warning. They were recent pictures. He had your wedding picture too."

"My what? Who gave it to him? Mom, I suppose."

"Janet, he went to your wedding, to the church that is."

"How was that possible?"

"He said he wouldn't have missed it for the world."

"Wait a minute. Could it have been him then? It must have been."

"Who?"

"Andrew and I received on our wedding day a big basket of white roses with a thousand-pound gift certificate from Harrods. There was no signature or name on the card. We couldn't figure out who could have given us such a generous gift and forgot to sign his name."

"I'm sure it was Daddy. You want me to ask him?"

"No, don't. Why? Are you going to see him again?"

"I might. Do you want to join me?"

"No thank you."

Mary surprised Arthur by showing up for his next wine party with her cello. During the preceding month, Didi and Arthur took Mary out to dinner and the theater, and she babysat once for Eddy. She wanted to respond in the way she knew best—playing music for them and their guests during the wine party. Her performance added charm to the evening, and with all the appreciation she received, she resolved that once in a while, she would repeat that gesture.

Didi called Mary the following day. "I can't thank you enough for what you did yesterday. Everybody was thrilled, and most of all your father, but on top of that, it was a superb performance. Arthur was hoping against hope that Janet would turn up or contact him. I guess that won't happen. Be frank with me, Mary. Does she really want to sever ties with him?"

"When Janet first found out what had happened, she resented Daddy a lot. She felt she had been made a fool of going on her honeymoon to Mindanao and laying flowers on a grave bearing a fake name."

"She did that? I didn't know."

"Yes, she traced the house where he lived and met a woman who at first told her he was away and then got confused and said she'd made a mistake."

"Oh no! Mary, that was my house. She probably spoke to my mother. Now I understand the situation much better."

"Janet felt that everybody was hiding something from her. She had to find out the truth herself, the hard way, when she went to see the solicitor, who told her of the divorce settlement. It was the first time she knew that Mom and Dad were divorced and that he was alive. She turned bitter, but I'm sure she'll mellow in time."

"Mary, I want very much to meet her. Can you arrange it?"

"I don't think that's a good idea, Didi. She resents you too I have to say."

"She doesn't need to know who I am, and I won't raise the issue with her. I simply want to know if she'll accept me as a friend. Why don't you invite her to your apartment for a wine and cheese party and ask me and a couple of other friends of yours to come and then leave it to me from there on?"

"How can I introduce you? She knows your name, and if she finds out my role in arranging this encounter, she'll turn against me as well."

"You can introduce me using my real name, Dolores,

one of your music fans. I won't talk about your father or our relations I promise."

Two weeks passed before Mary found the courage and the time to organize her party. Apart from Janet and Didi, two classmates—an Irishman and a Canadian—were also invited. Didi brought three bottles of wine, and Mary provided cheese and crackers. Mary was nervous at first, but noting the ease with which her guests blended, she began to relax.

Janet and Didi talked about Manila—the city, the shopping, the people, and the food—and exchanged information on what their husbands were doing. The other three congregated at one point to talk about the academy and the upcoming musical events. Janet found herself warming up to Dolores. By the time they were about to leave, she and Dolores had exchanged phone numbers.

"I come down to London once in a while. If you happen to be free then, maybe we can see each other for tea," said Didi.

"I'd like that."

For the next couple of months, Didi kept in touch with Janet. On one occasion, she invited her, Andrew, and Mary to a Chinese restaurant. Didi showed up alone apologizing that her husband had come down with the flu. As a matter of fact, Arthur had been kept in the dark about his wife's contact with Janet; Didi wanted to spare him a frustrated attempt at reconciliation with his daughter. The four enjoyed that evening. Didi proved herself once more to be a charming hostess, and the food was excellent.

"A delightful evening," Andrew said to Janet as they drove home.

"Isn't she lovely?" Janet asked.

"She is. She was elegantly dressed, intelligent, and good company."

Janet and Didi went out for coffee or joined each other's company on their shopping sprees once every ten days or so. Then the day came when Didi felt it was time to touch on the subject she had been longing to discuss with Janet.

"Tell me, Janet. You mentioned you went to Mindanao for a day. This is too short a period to see the island properly. Do you know that I was born and lived there for a while? That is, before moving to Manila?"

"I didn't know. Actually, Andrew and I weren't sightseeing. My father spent well over a year on the island, and I thought he had died and was buried there. We sort of went to visit his grave."

Didi kept silent. Janet went on to reveal to her newfound friend her ordeal and how she had come to resent her father and above all the girl he had married.

"If I understood you correctly, your father took on the identity of another person because he was in love with a woman and wanted to free himself to marry her. Now Janet, you're studying to become a lawyer. If you were to defend him, how would you plead his case?"

Janet was taken by surprise. "Well, I haven't thought about it. A crime of passion I suppose."

"Why do you call it a crime? Did your father kill or steal from anybody?"

"No, but taking another person's identity is forgery."

"Forgive me, Janet. I'm not as educated as you are. I didn't go beyond high school. I know nothing about legal matters, but if he'd used the identity of another person to defraud him of his possessions, he would have committed forgery, but simply living under another name, a dead man's name in this case, need not really be a crime. After all, there are so many people who live under assumed names. Take film stars for example. If they can do it, why not other people as well? No, I believe what you have against him most is that his love for the other person has replaced his love for his family and more particularly for you and Mary, but even that you don't know for sure."

"I must admit that when Mary visited him, she told me that he had my picture in his living room and that he'd gone to my wedding."

"Janet, I'm happy you confided in me. It's time I go. Once more, it was lovely being with you. I'll be in touch."

A week passed since Janet had last seen Dolores. She thought often of their last discussion. The challenge handed to her of defending her father was daunting, but it was legitimate. After all, lawyers were meant to defend the guilty more often than the innocent. *But what was the real guilt of her father?* she asked herself. *Did his action really border on a criminal offense?* She was not sure anymore.

It was early afternoon when Janet returned home one day and sorted through her mail, which included a handwritten envelope addressed to her. She opened it glancing quickly at the signature. It was from Dolores. *How strange. Why did she write instead of phoning?* She sat and read it.

My dear Janet,

It never occurred to me in my wildest dreams that one day you and Andrew would be knocking at the door of our family home in Mindanao. That house holds so many memories for me. It is where I grew up and where your father and I met and fell in love. It was also from that house that we embarked on what my brother Miguel described as a road of no return.

At the time, we were so preoccupied with our own future life that we overlooked the suffering we caused you and others. Many years have passed since we took that road, an arduous journey for your father, who had to live in his own shadow for so long and be made to believe that he had been cast away from your life for good. Can we be forgiven? If not me, can you at all help your father come in from the cold?

I want to apologize for disguising my true identity till now. Believe me, it was not out of malice. I was simply too afraid to be rejected outright. I wanted to win you over, but the more we met, the more I came to like and admire you. Eventually, your friendship became more important than winning you over to one point of view or another. If you decide to sever our relationship, that is your privilege, but I will always cherish our friendship.

By the time you receive this letter, our little boy, Eddy, will have been operated on at St. Mary's Hospital. He was born with a defective heart valve. The operation will take place on Monday. For months, we have been in agony and praying for his safety. The doctor is reassuring, but with open-heart surgery, anything can happen. Pray with us, Janet, if you will.

As ever, yours,
Dolores

Janet gazed into space for a moment as if waking up from a dream. She looked at her watch. It was Thursday, so the operation had taken place three days earlier. She wanted to call Dolores and get the news. *Oh God! I hope it went all right,* she thought. No one answered the phone. *But of course. Silly me. She must be at the hospital.* She had never met Eddy, but she felt that a bond had developed between them.

The door of the room at the hospital opened gently. Little Eddy was in bed having left intensive care that morning. Didi stood and looked at Janet with anxious eyes. Janet hugged her with wet eyes asking her about the operation. Didi said, "It went all right. He'll be OK."

"I'm so relieved." She produced a stuffed dinosaur. "This is for you, Eddy. Do you know who I am?" Eddy shook his head. "I'm your sister, Janet." She disregarded the puzzled look on the boy's face.

"I got your letter, Didi. I'm so happy to know that Dolores and Didi are one and the same because I'm very fond of Dolores."

They were wiping their tears when they were interrupted by a brief knock. The door gently opened. Arthur stood there in disbelief. "Janet?"

She rushed to him with open arms tears still flowing.

"Oh Daddy! Welcome back!"

Epilogue

Over the following couple of months, Janet and Arthur met several times. She told him that it felt a bit strange calling him Daddy when she hardly knew him. As a child, she dreamed of him coming back with lots of stories about his life overseas. Now that he was back, she wanted to hear it all. This would gradually bring them closer.

Arthur answered her many questions particularly about the plot to fake his death. Out of respect and growing affection for him and Didi, she did not want to dwell on the why but on how it had been done.

"Daddy, I've been thinking," Janet said one day. "There's still one bit of unfinished business. It relates to the real Arturo Fernandez. Don't you think you owe it to his family to let them know of his gravesite and have it correctly marked?"

"I think of that once in a while and feel guilty about it," Arthur said. "You're right. I need to set the record straight. How I don't know. I'll write Miguel. He's resourceful. Perhaps he can find a way."

Acknowledgments

On several occasions during my international career, I moved family and home from one country and continent to another. My late wife, Georgette, embraced every move with enthusiasm and immersed herself in the newfound cultures. My two sons, Kevin O'Leary and Shane O'Leary, also readily accepted the challenge of repeatedly facing new schools and starting new friendships. I am eternally grateful for their support in fostering my career and for enabling me to pursue my interests in such areas as writing.

I am also grateful to Nicole Zakher for graciously volunteering to type this novel's manuscript.